MANGA MATH MYSTERIES #5

THE ANCIENT FORMULA

A Mystery with Fractions

by Melinda Thielbar

illustrated by Tintin Pantoja

GRAPHIC UNIVERSE™ · MINNEAPOLIS · NEW YORK

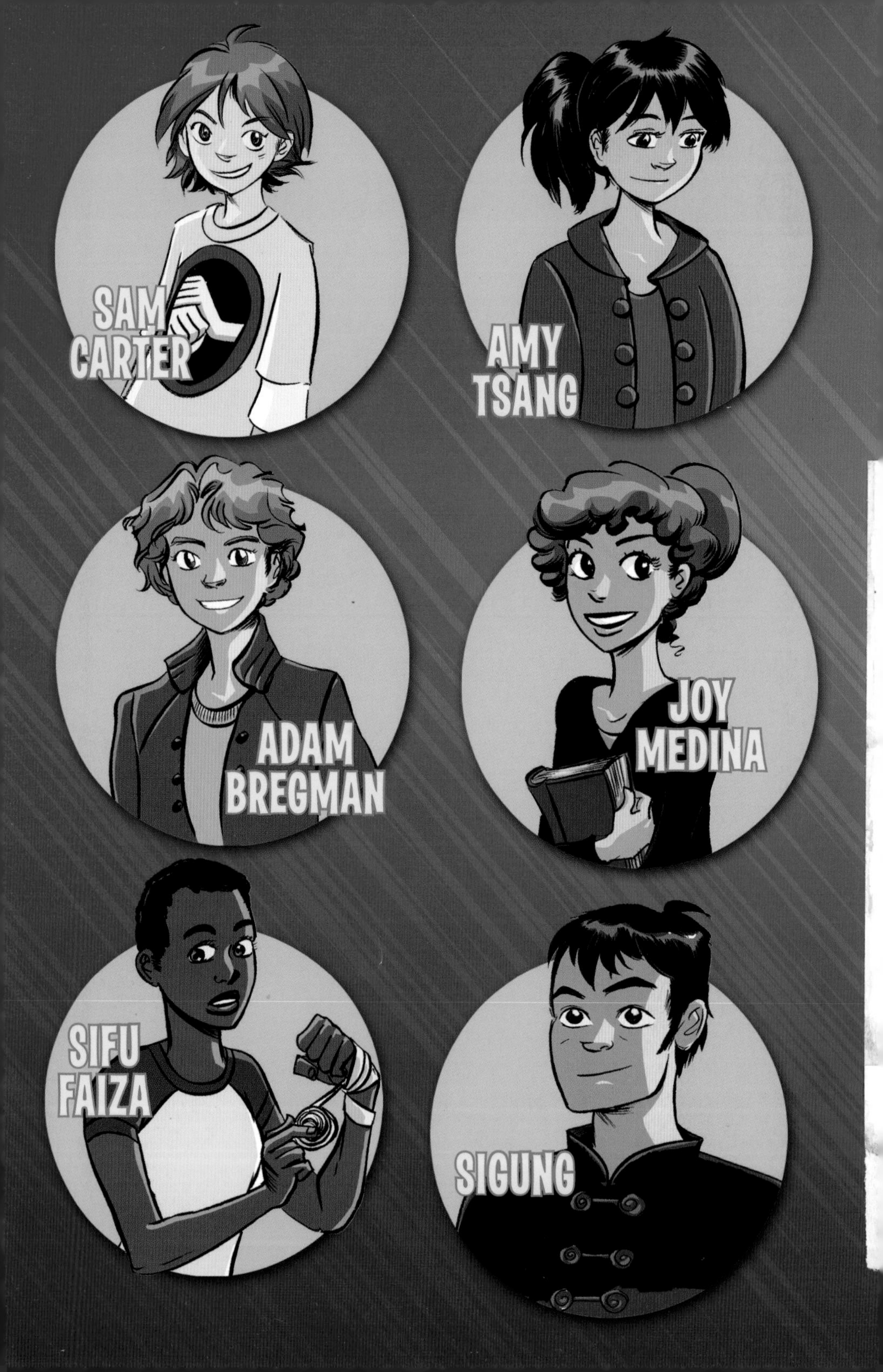
SAM CARTER
AMY TSANG
ADAM BREGMAN
JOY MEDINA
SIFU FAIZA
SIGUNG

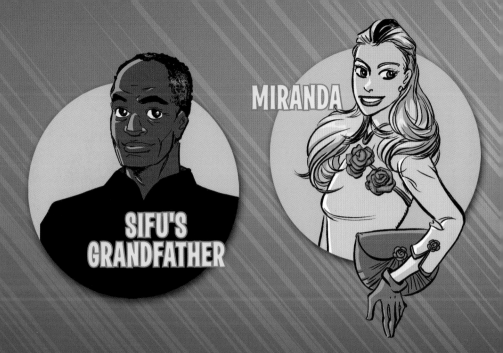

SIFU'S GRANDFATHER

MIRANDA

What are fractions? Fractions are numbers that show parts of a whole. We write fractions with two numbers, one above the other. The top number is the numerator. It tells how many equal parts we have. The bottom number is the denominator. It tells how many equal parts make up 1 whole. When fractions have the same denominator, we can add and subtract them. And we can write 1 whole as any fraction with the same numerator and denominator:

$$\frac{1}{4} + \frac{3}{4} = \frac{1+3}{4} = \frac{4}{4} = 1$$

We use fractions all the time. We use them to divide a pie or a pizza into slices of equal size. We also use them in cooking when a recipe calls for $\frac{1}{2}$ cup or $\frac{1}{4}$ teaspoon. We even use them in telling time!

Story by Melinda Thielbar
Pencils and inks by Tintin Pantoja
Coloring by Hi-Fi Design
Lettering by Marshall Dillon

Copyright © 2011 by Lerner Publishing Group, Inc.

Graphic Universe™ is a trademark of Lerner Publishing Group, Inc.

Graphic Universe™
A division of Lerner Publishing Group, Inc.
241 First Avenue North
Minneapolis, MN 55401 U.S.A.

Website address: www.lernerbooks.com

Library of Congress Cataloging-in-Publication Data

Thielbar, Melinda.
     The ancient formula : a mystery with fractions / by Melinda Thielbar ;
  illustrated by Tintin Pantoja.
         p.   cm. — (Manga math mysteries ; #5)
     Summary: The students of Sifu Faiza's Kung Fu School use their knowledge of
  fractions as they try to discover what happened to Leung Jan's long-lost healing
  formula.
     ISBN: 978–0–7613–4907–5 (lib. bdg. : alk. paper)
     1. Graphic novels. [1. Graphic novels. 2. Mystery and detective stories.
  3. Mathematics—Fiction. 4. Kung fu—Fiction. 5. Schools—Fiction.] I. Pantoja,
  Tintin, ill. II. Title.
  PZ7.7.T48Anc 2011
  741.5'973—dc22   2010001431

Manufactured in the United States of America
1 – DP – 7/15/10

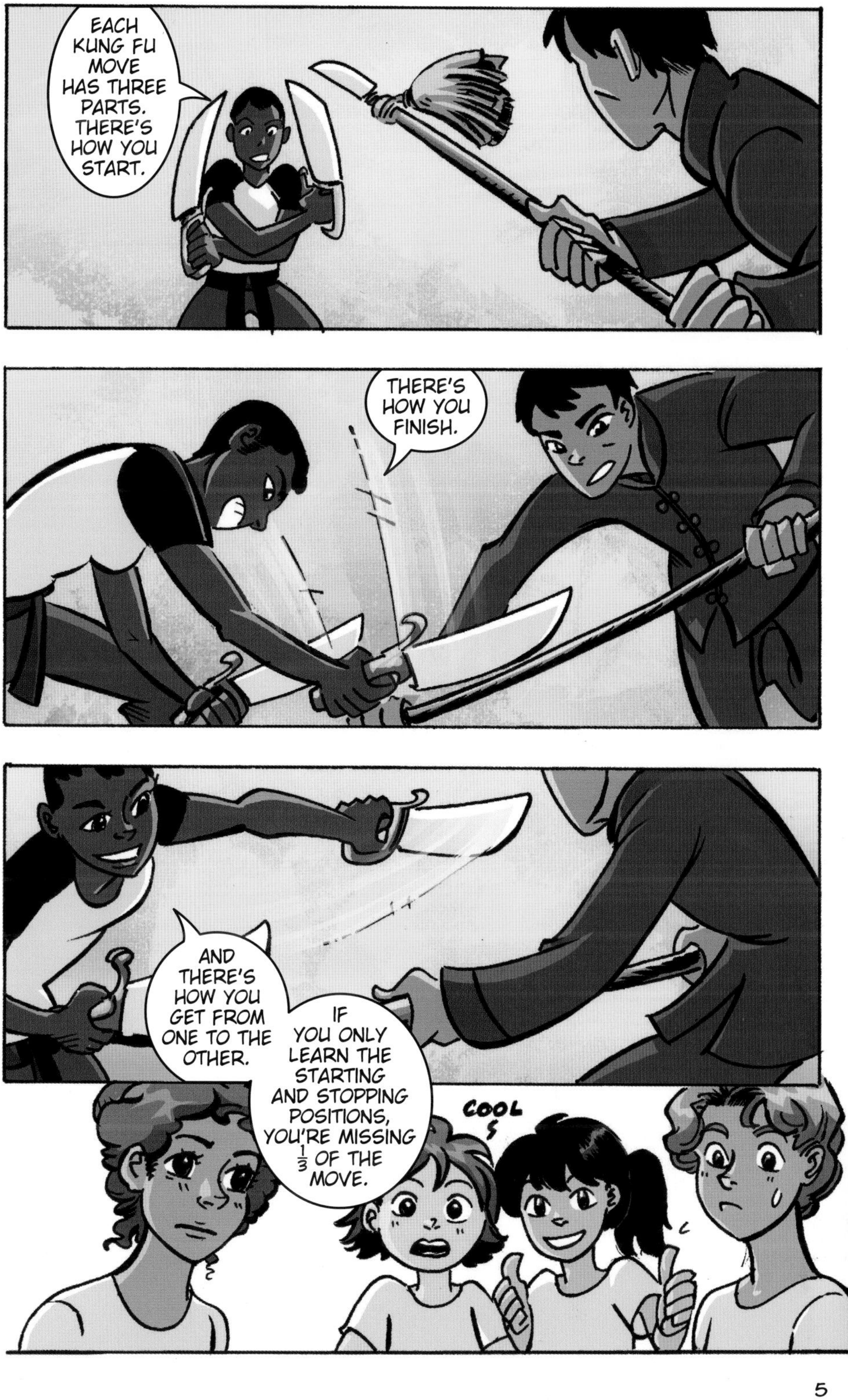
EACH KUNG FU MOVE HAS THREE PARTS. THERE'S HOW YOU START.
THERE'S HOW YOU FINISH.
AND THERE'S HOW YOU GET FROM ONE TO THE OTHER.
IF YOU ONLY LEARN THE STARTING AND STOPPING POSITIONS, YOU'RE MISSING $\frac{1}{3}$ OF THE MOVE.
COOL

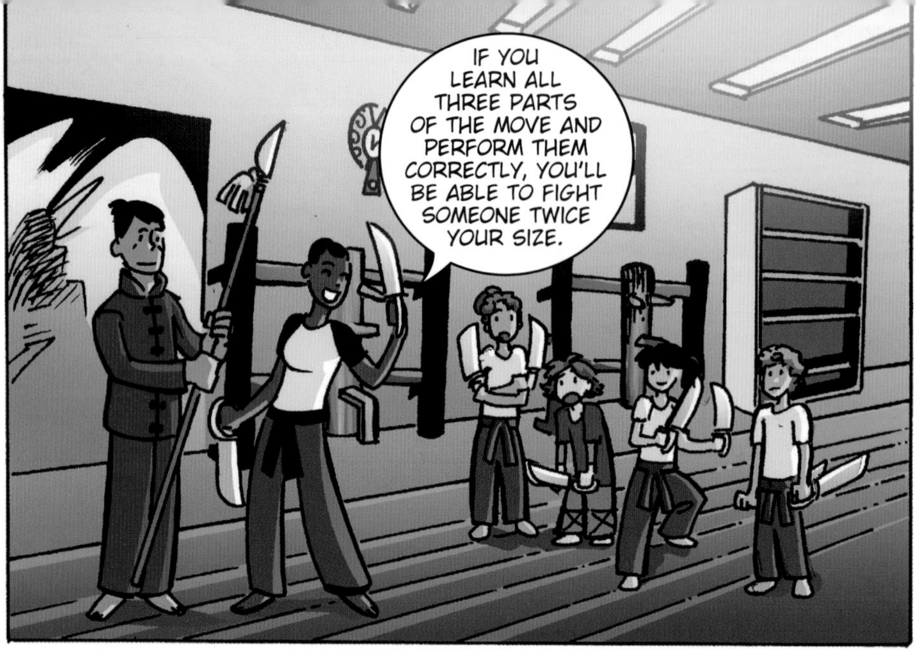
IF YOU LEARN ALL THREE PARTS OF THE MOVE AND PERFORM THEM CORRECTLY, YOU'LL BE ABLE TO FIGHT SOMEONE TWICE YOUR SIZE.

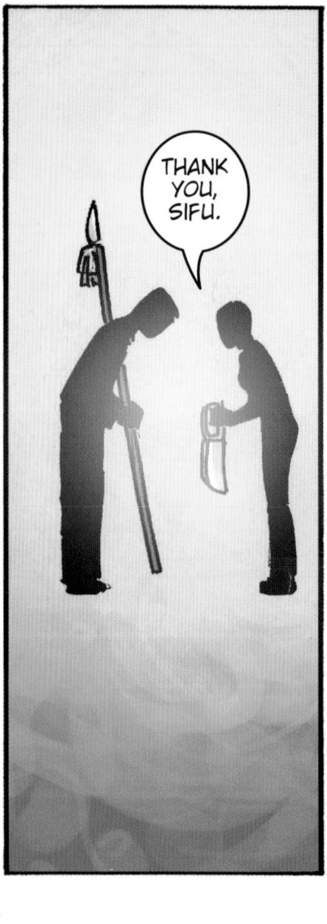
THANK YOU, SIFU.

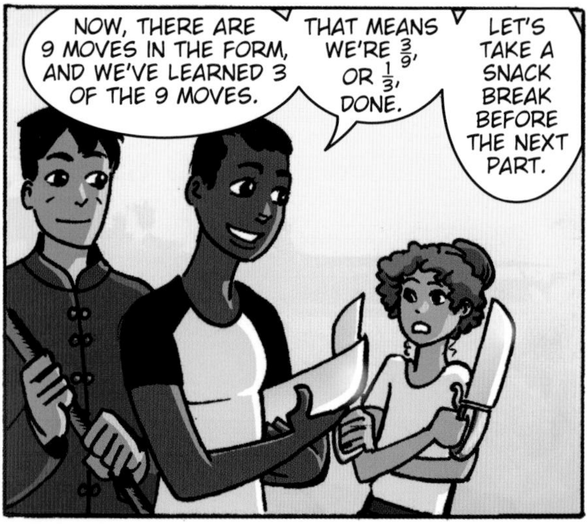
NOW, THERE ARE 9 MOVES IN THE FORM, AND WE'VE LEARNED 3 OF THE 9 MOVES.
THAT MEANS WE'RE $\frac{3}{9}$, OR $\frac{1}{3}$, DONE.
LET'S TAKE A SNACK BREAK BEFORE THE NEXT PART.

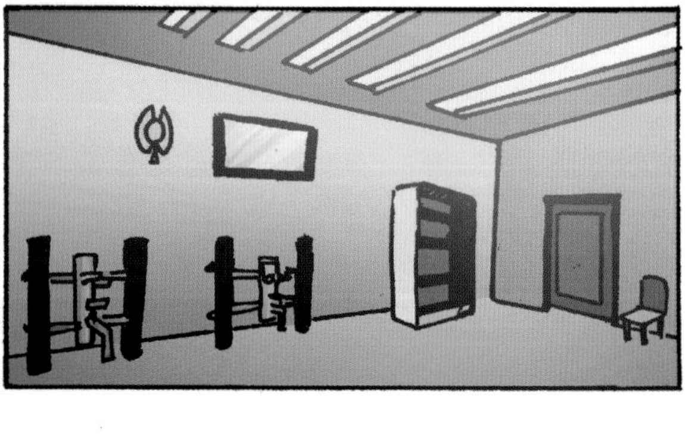

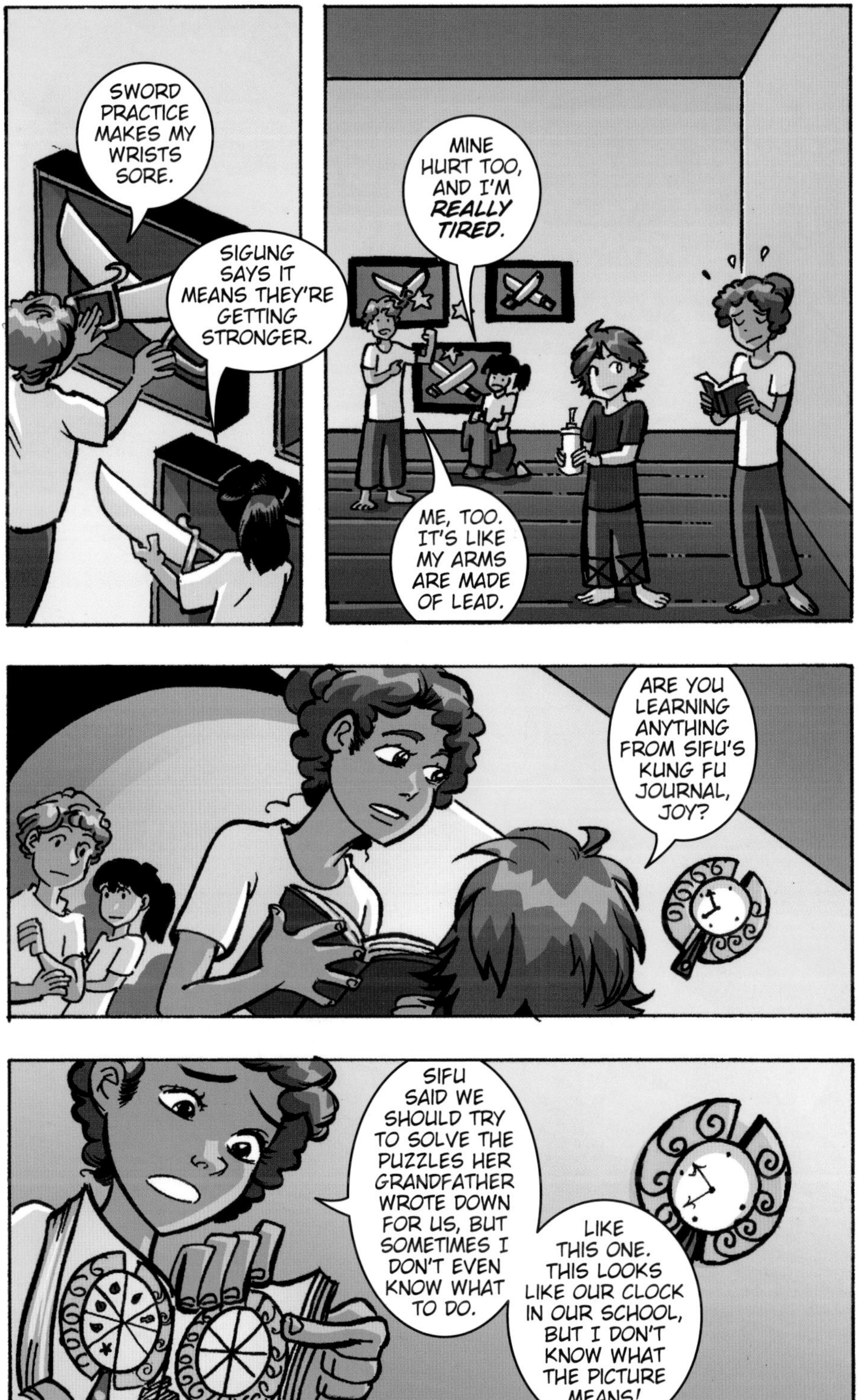
SWORD PRACTICE MAKES MY WRISTS SORE.
SIGUNG SAYS IT MEANS THEY'RE GETTING STRONGER.
MINE HURT TOO, AND I'M *REALLY TIRED*.
ME, TOO. IT'S LIKE MY ARMS ARE MADE OF LEAD.
ARE YOU LEARNING ANYTHING FROM SIFU'S KUNG FU JOURNAL, JOY?
SIFU SAID WE SHOULD TRY TO SOLVE THE PUZZLES HER GRANDFATHER WROTE DOWN FOR US, BUT SOMETIMES I DON'T EVEN KNOW WHAT TO DO.
LIKE THIS ONE. THIS LOOKS LIKE OUR CLOCK IN OUR SCHOOL, BUT I DON'T KNOW WHAT THE PICTURE MEANS!

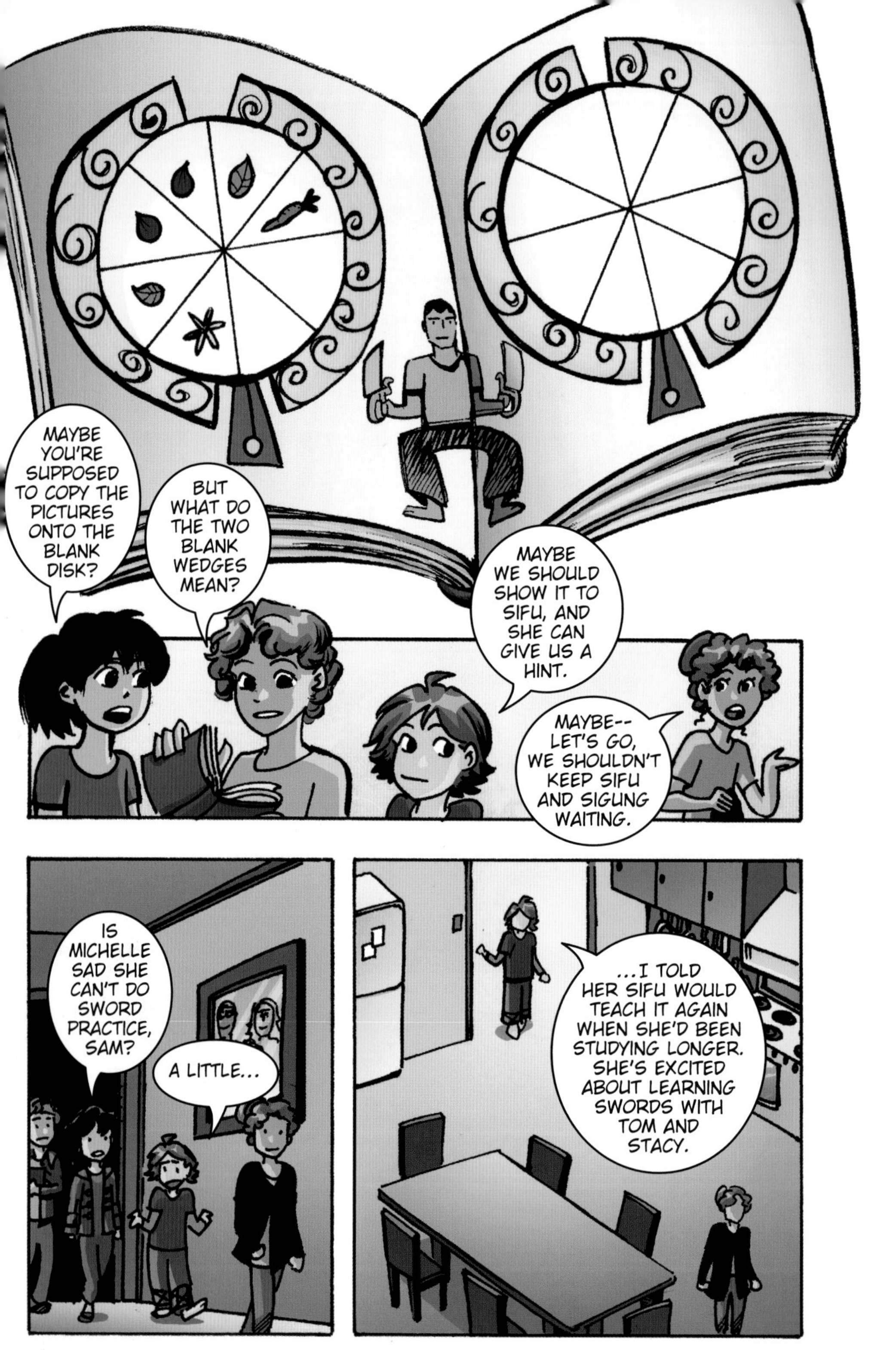
MAYBE YOU'RE SUPPOSED TO COPY THE PICTURES ONTO THE BLANK DISK?
BUT WHAT DO THE TWO BLANK WEDGES MEAN?
MAYBE WE SHOULD SHOW IT TO SIFU, AND SHE CAN GIVE US A HINT.
MAYBE-- LET'S GO, WE SHOULDN'T KEEP SIFU AND SIGUNG WAITING.
IS MICHELLE SAD SHE CAN'T DO SWORD PRACTICE, SAM?
A LITTLE...
...I TOLD HER SIFU WOULD TEACH IT AGAIN WHEN SHE'D BEEN STUDYING LONGER. SHE'S EXCITED ABOUT LEARNING SWORDS WITH TOM AND STACY.

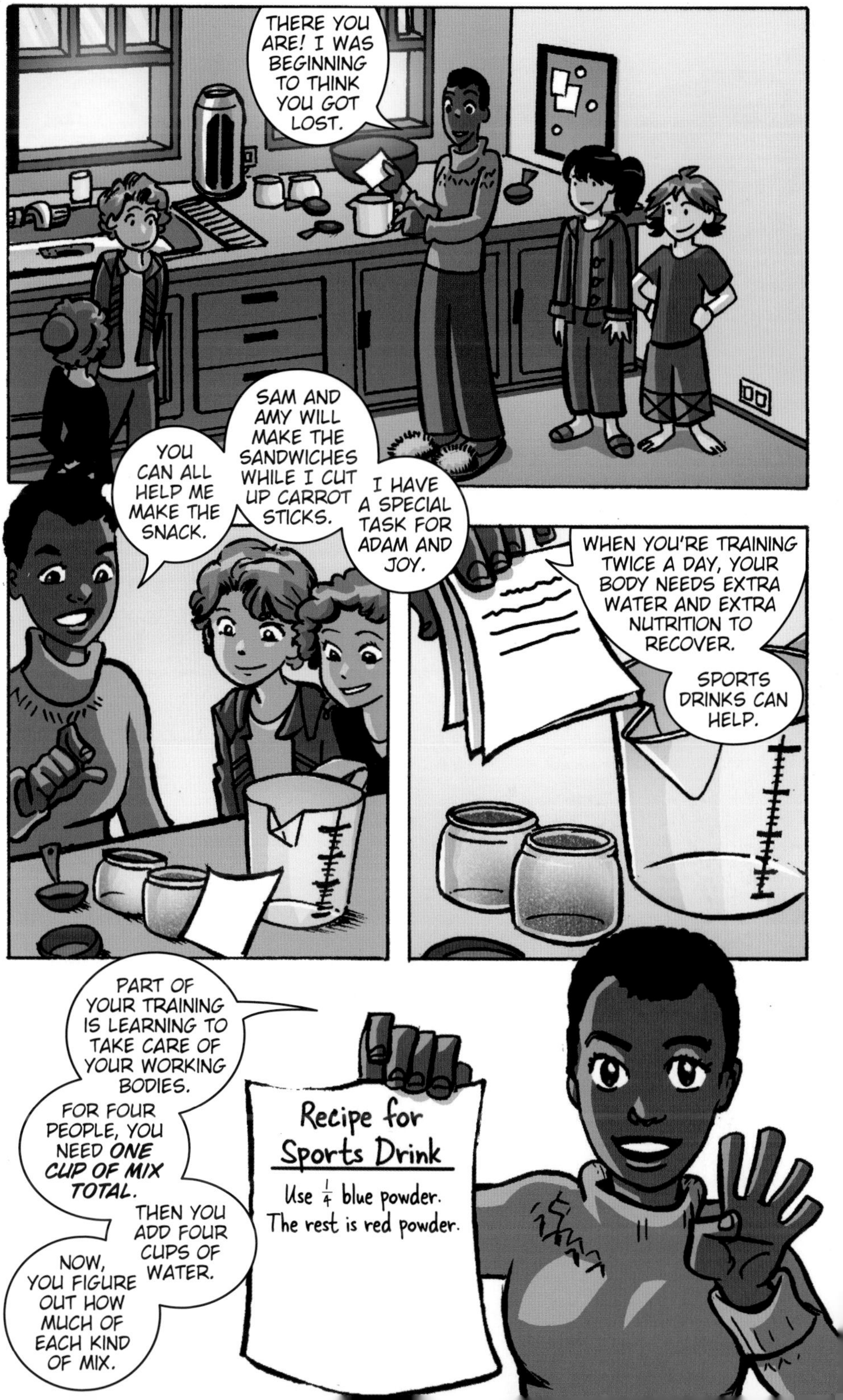
THERE YOU ARE! I WAS BEGINNING TO THINK YOU GOT LOST.
YOU CAN ALL HELP ME MAKE THE SNACK.
SAM AND AMY WILL MAKE THE SANDWICHES WHILE I CUT UP CARROT STICKS.
I HAVE A SPECIAL TASK FOR ADAM AND JOY.
WHEN YOU'RE TRAINING TWICE A DAY, YOUR BODY NEEDS EXTRA WATER AND EXTRA NUTRITION TO RECOVER.
SPORTS DRINKS CAN HELP.
PART OF YOUR TRAINING IS LEARNING TO TAKE CARE OF YOUR WORKING BODIES.
FOR FOUR PEOPLE, YOU NEED ***ONE CUP OF MIX TOTAL***.
THEN YOU ADD FOUR CUPS OF WATER.
NOW, YOU FIGURE OUT HOW MUCH OF EACH KIND OF MIX.
Recipe for Sports Drink
Use $\frac{1}{4}$ blue powder.
The rest is red powder.

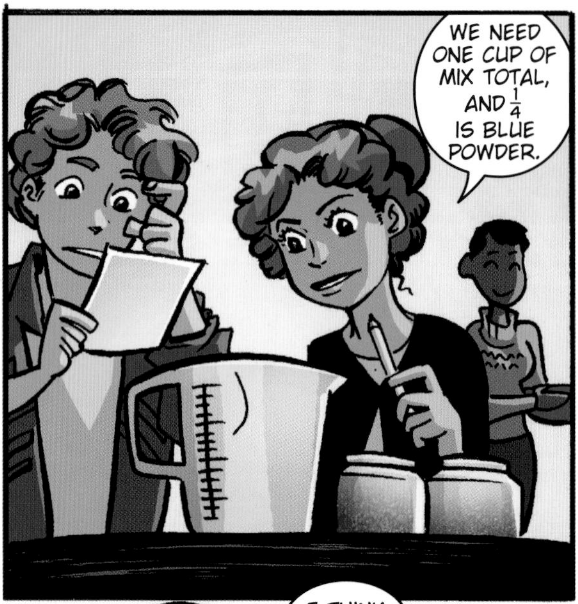
WE NEED ONE CUP OF MIX TOTAL, AND $\frac{1}{4}$ IS BLUE POWDER.

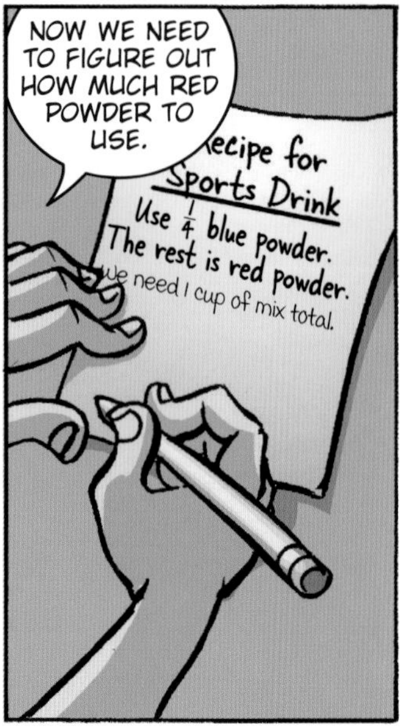
NOW WE NEED TO FIGURE OUT HOW MUCH RED POWDER TO USE.
ecipe for
Sports Drink
Use $\frac{1}{4}$ blue powder.
The rest is red powder.
e need 1 cup of mix total.

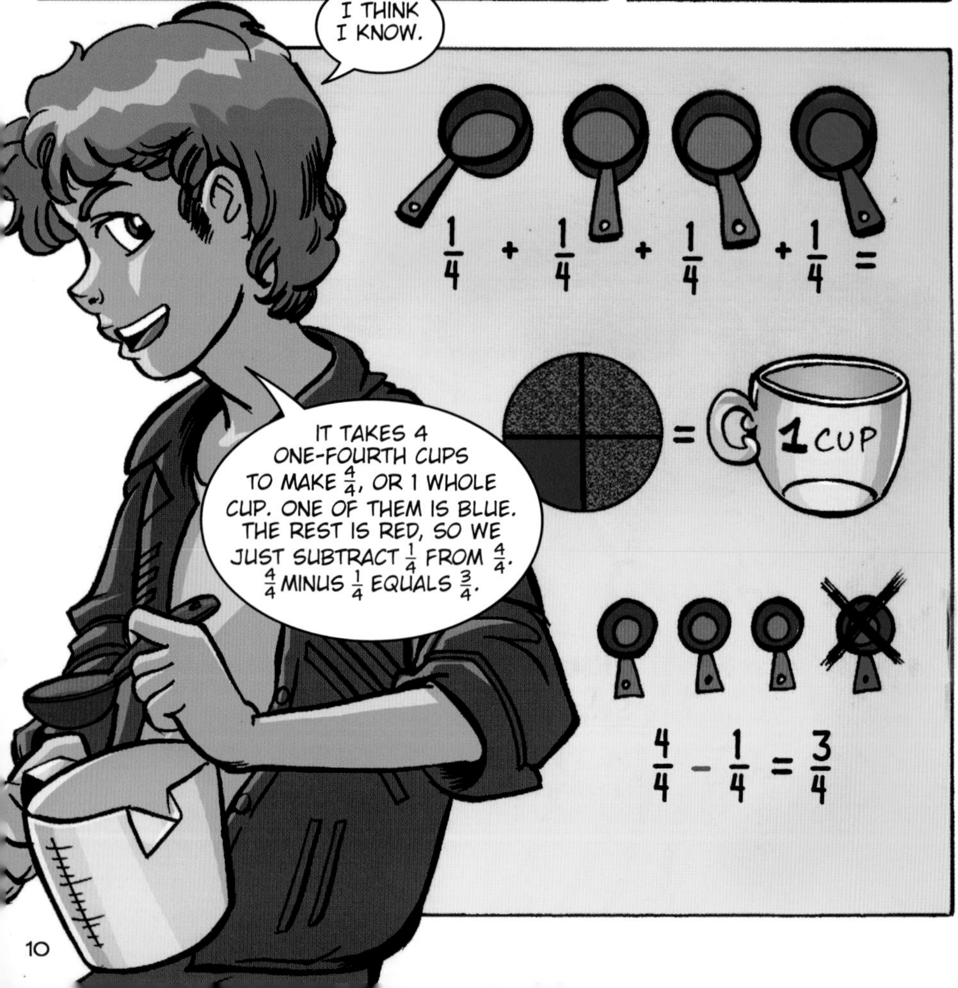
I THINK I KNOW.
$\frac{1}{4} + \frac{1}{4} + \frac{1}{4} + \frac{1}{4} =$
= 1 CUP
IT TAKES 4 ONE-FOURTH CUPS TO MAKE $\frac{4}{4}$, OR 1 WHOLE CUP. ONE OF THEM IS BLUE. THE REST IS RED, SO WE JUST SUBTRACT $\frac{1}{4}$ FROM $\frac{4}{4}$. $\frac{4}{4}$ MINUS $\frac{1}{4}$ EQUALS $\frac{3}{4}$.
$\frac{4}{4} - \frac{1}{4} = \frac{3}{4}$

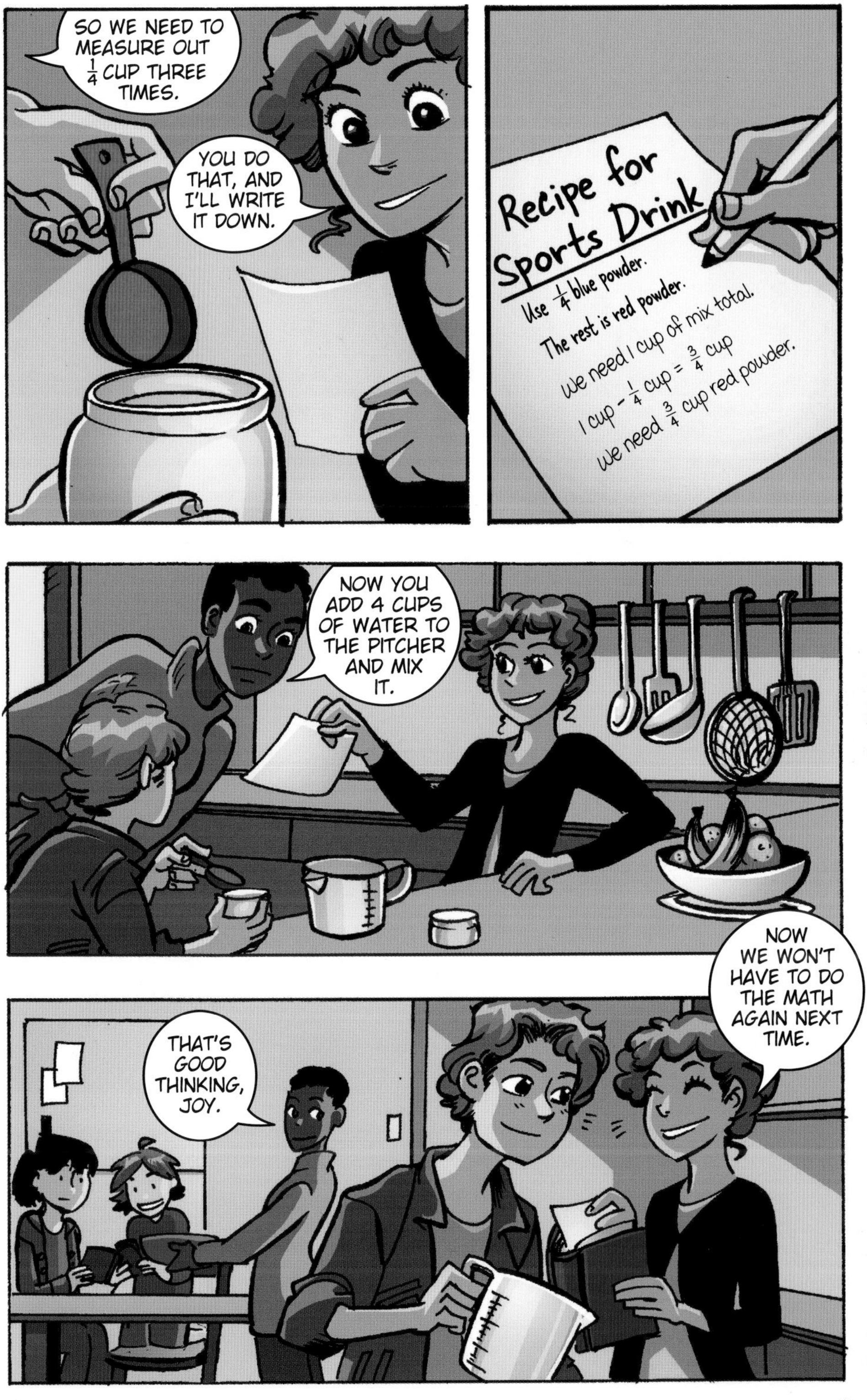
SO WE NEED TO MEASURE OUT $\frac{1}{4}$ CUP THREE TIMES.
YOU DO THAT, AND I'LL WRITE IT DOWN.
Recipe for Sports Drink
Use $\frac{1}{4}$ blue powder.
The rest is red powder.
we need 1 cup of mix total.
1 cup - $\frac{1}{4}$ cup = $\frac{3}{4}$ cup
we need $\frac{3}{4}$ cup red powder.
NOW YOU ADD 4 CUPS OF WATER TO THE PITCHER AND MIX IT.
THAT'S GOOD THINKING, JOY.
NOW WE WON'T HAVE TO DO THE MATH AGAIN NEXT TIME.

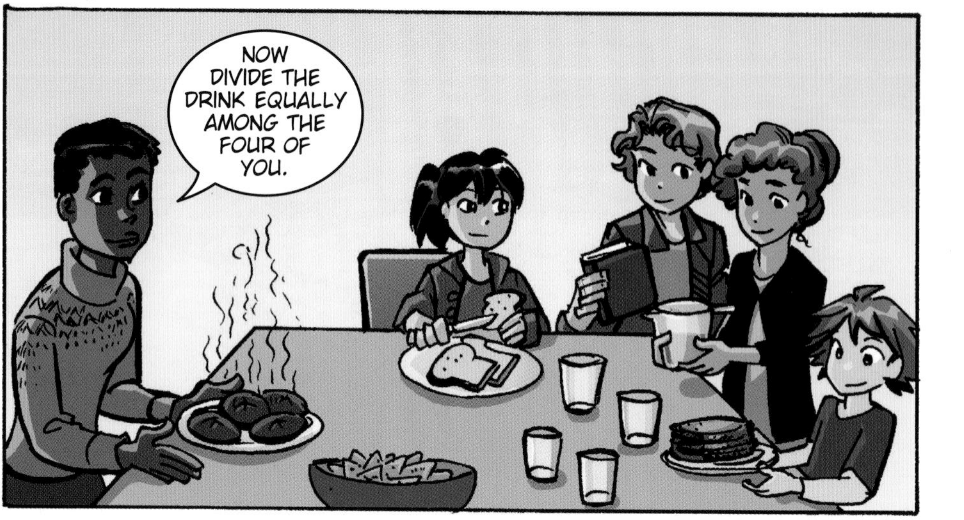
NOW DIVIDE THE DRINK EQUALLY AMONG THE FOUR OF YOU.

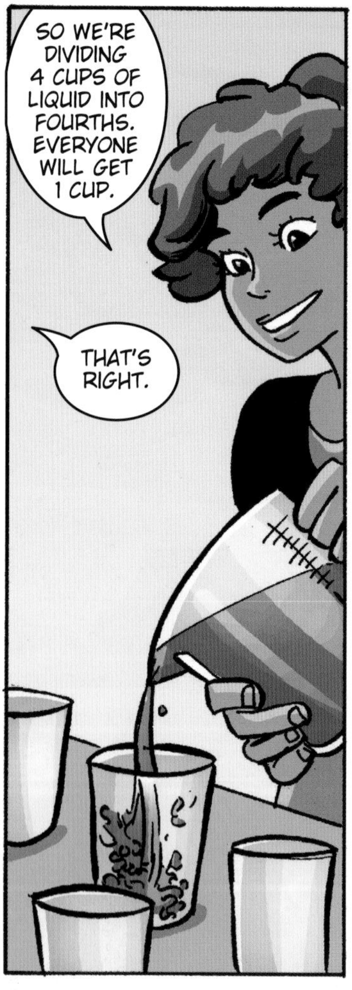
SO WE'RE DIVIDING 4 CUPS OF LIQUID INTO FOURTHS. EVERYONE WILL GET 1 CUP.
THAT'S RIGHT.

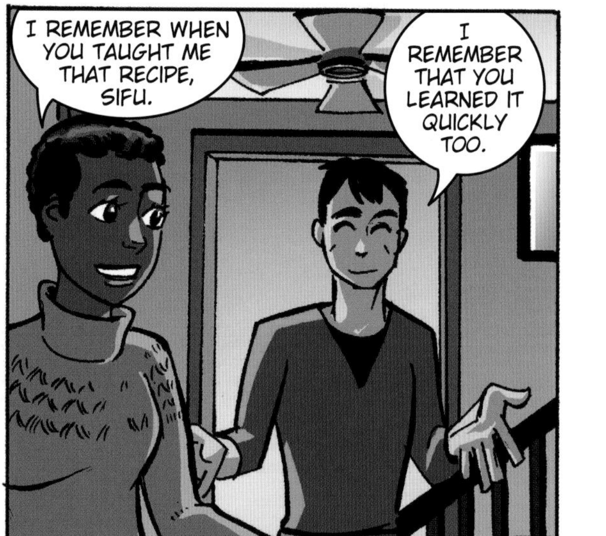
I REMEMBER WHEN YOU TAUGHT ME THAT RECIPE, SIFU.
I REMEMBER THAT YOU LEARNED IT QUICKLY TOO.

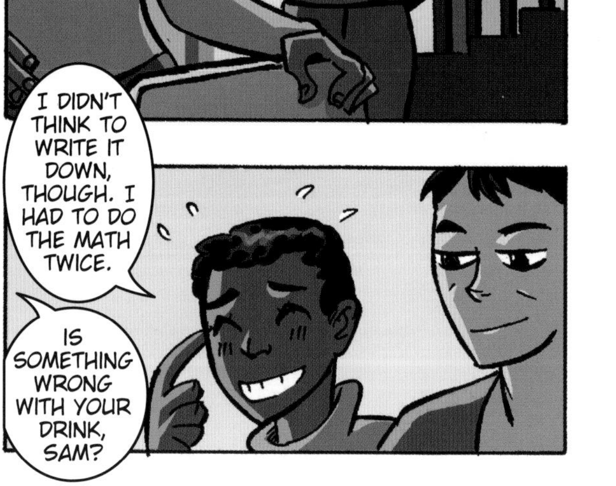
I DIDN'T THINK TO WRITE IT DOWN, THOUGH. I HAD TO DO THE MATH TWICE.
IS SOMETHING WRONG WITH YOUR DRINK, SAM?

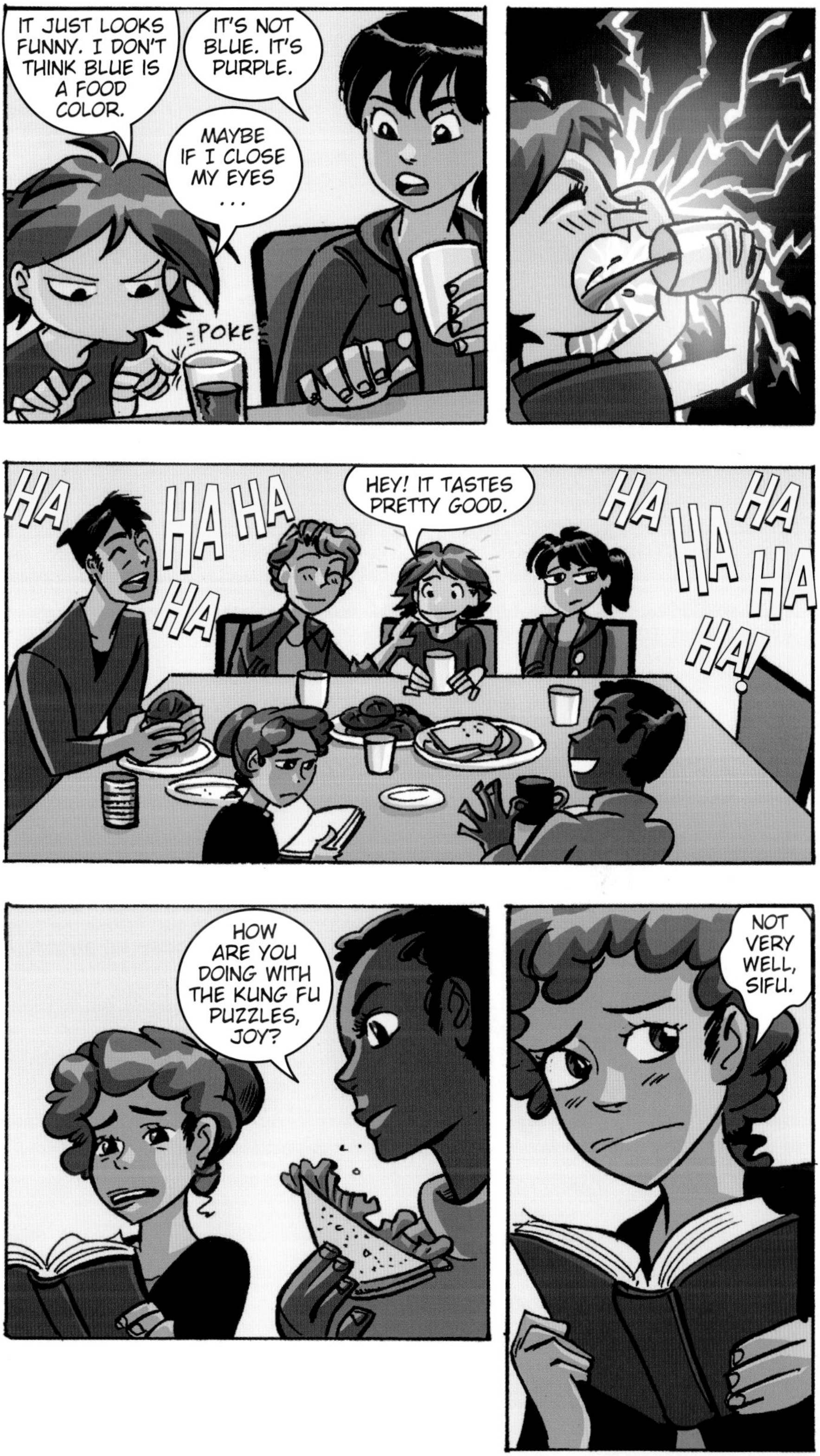
IT JUST LOOKS FUNNY. I DON'T THINK BLUE IS A FOOD COLOR.
IT'S NOT BLUE. IT'S PURPLE.
MAYBE IF I CLOSE MY EYES . . .
POKE
HA HA HA HA
HEY! IT TASTES PRETTY GOOD.
HA HA HA HA HA HA!
HOW ARE YOU DOING WITH THE KUNG FU PUZZLES, JOY?
NOT VERY WELL, SIFU.

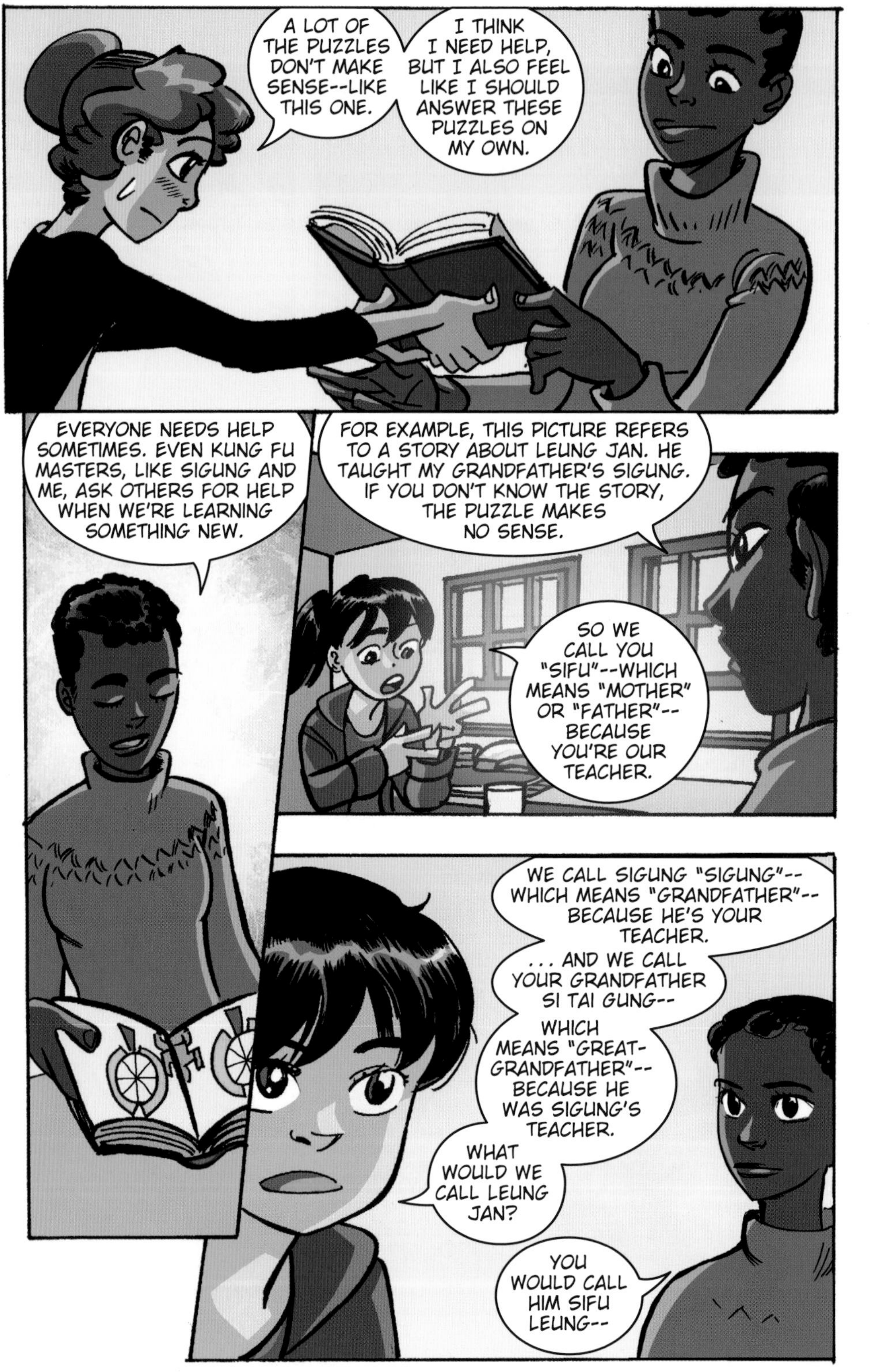
A LOT OF THE PUZZLES DON'T MAKE SENSE--LIKE THIS ONE.
I THINK I NEED HELP, BUT I ALSO FEEL LIKE I SHOULD ANSWER THESE PUZZLES ON MY OWN.
EVERYONE NEEDS HELP SOMETIMES. EVEN KUNG FU MASTERS, LIKE SIGUNG AND ME, ASK OTHERS FOR HELP WHEN WE'RE LEARNING SOMETHING NEW.
FOR EXAMPLE, THIS PICTURE REFERS TO A STORY ABOUT LEUNG JAN. HE TAUGHT MY GRANDFATHER'S SIGUNG. IF YOU DON'T KNOW THE STORY, THE PUZZLE MAKES NO SENSE.
SO WE CALL YOU "SIFU"--WHICH MEANS "MOTHER" OR "FATHER"--BECAUSE YOU'RE OUR TEACHER.
WE CALL SIGUNG "SIGUNG"--WHICH MEANS "GRANDFATHER"--BECAUSE HE'S YOUR TEACHER.
. . . AND WE CALL YOUR GRANDFATHER SI TAI GUNG--
WHICH MEANS "GREAT-GRANDFATHER"--BECAUSE HE WAS SIGUNG'S TEACHER.
WHAT WOULD WE CALL LEUNG JAN?
YOU WOULD CALL HIM SIFU LEUNG--

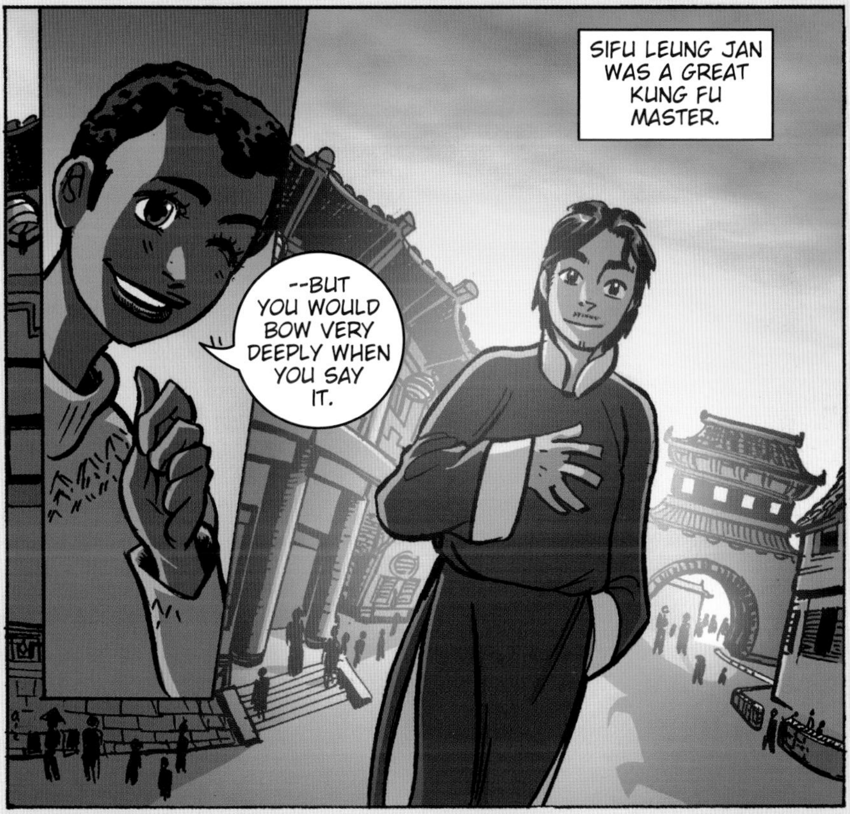

SIFU LEUNG JAN WAS A GREAT KUNG FU MASTER.
--BUT YOU WOULD BOW VERY DEEPLY WHEN YOU SAY IT.

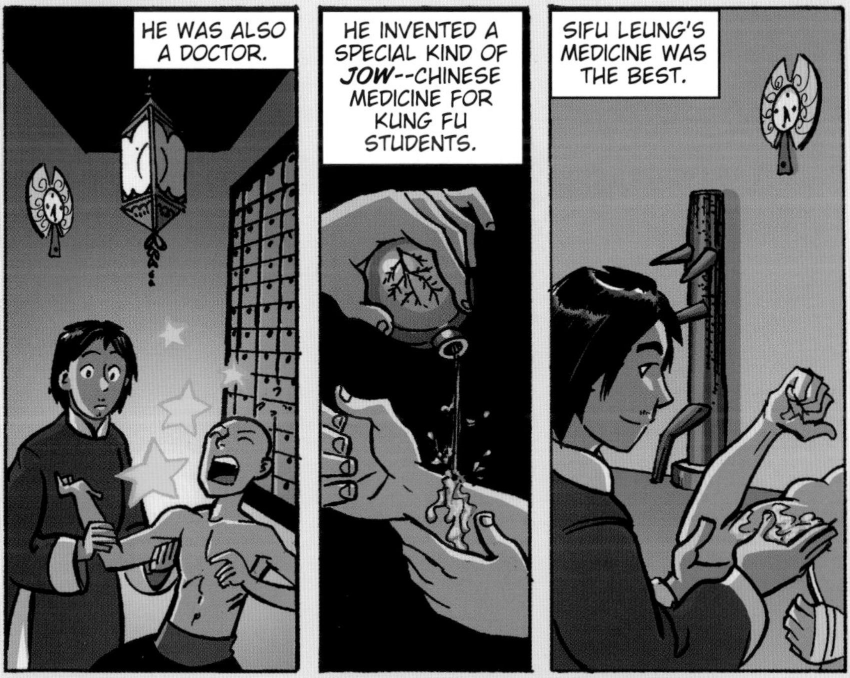

HE WAS ALSO A DOCTOR.
HE INVENTED A SPECIAL KIND OF ***JOW***--CHINESE MEDICINE FOR KUNG FU STUDENTS.
SIFU LEUNG'S MEDICINE WAS THE BEST.

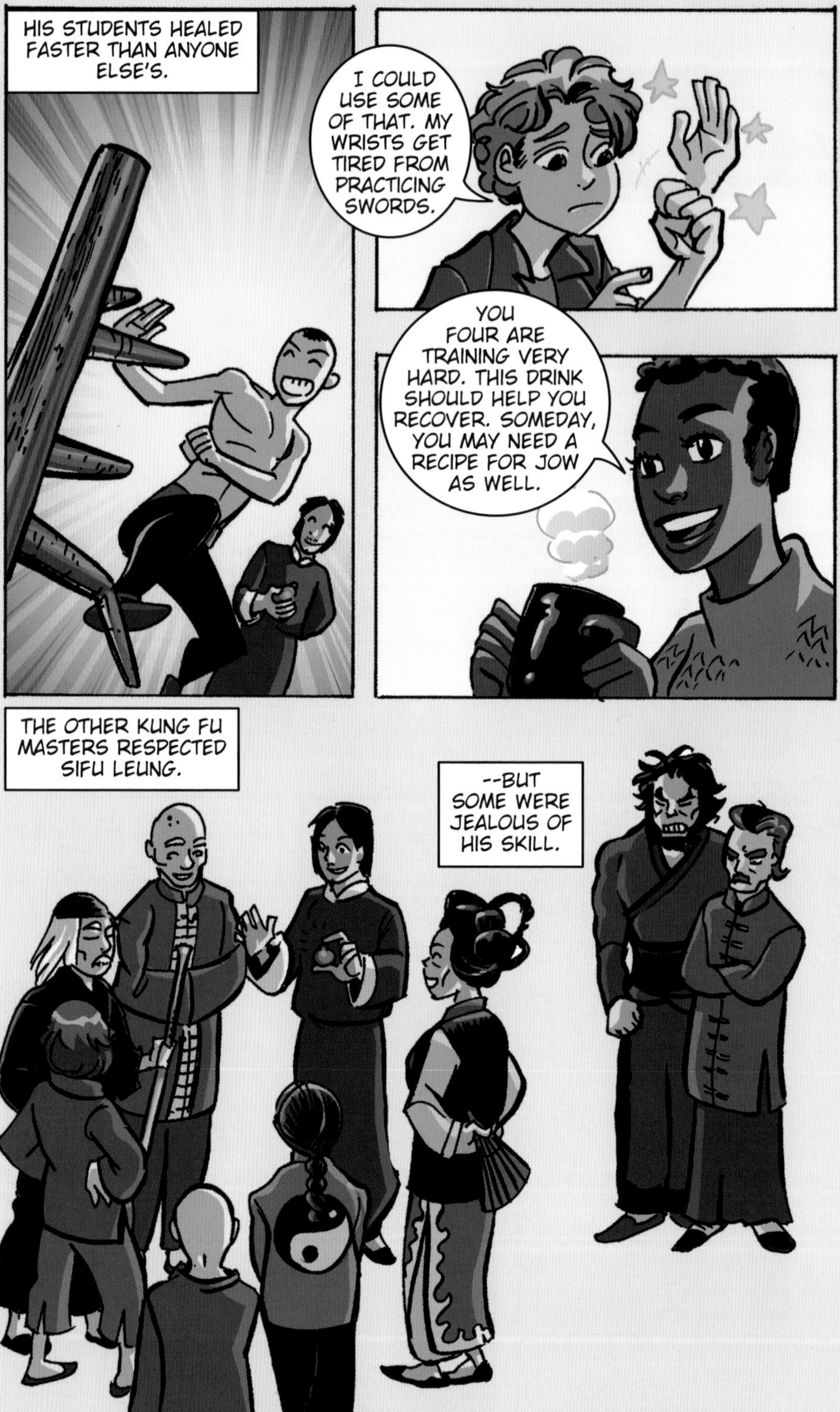
HIS STUDENTS HEALED FASTER THAN ANYONE ELSE'S.
I COULD USE SOME OF THAT. MY WRISTS GET TIRED FROM PRACTICING SWORDS.
YOU FOUR ARE TRAINING VERY HARD. THIS DRINK SHOULD HELP YOU RECOVER. SOMEDAY, YOU MAY NEED A RECIPE FOR JOW AS WELL.
THE OTHER KUNG FU MASTERS RESPECTED SIFU LEUNG.
--BUT SOME WERE JEALOUS OF HIS SKILL.

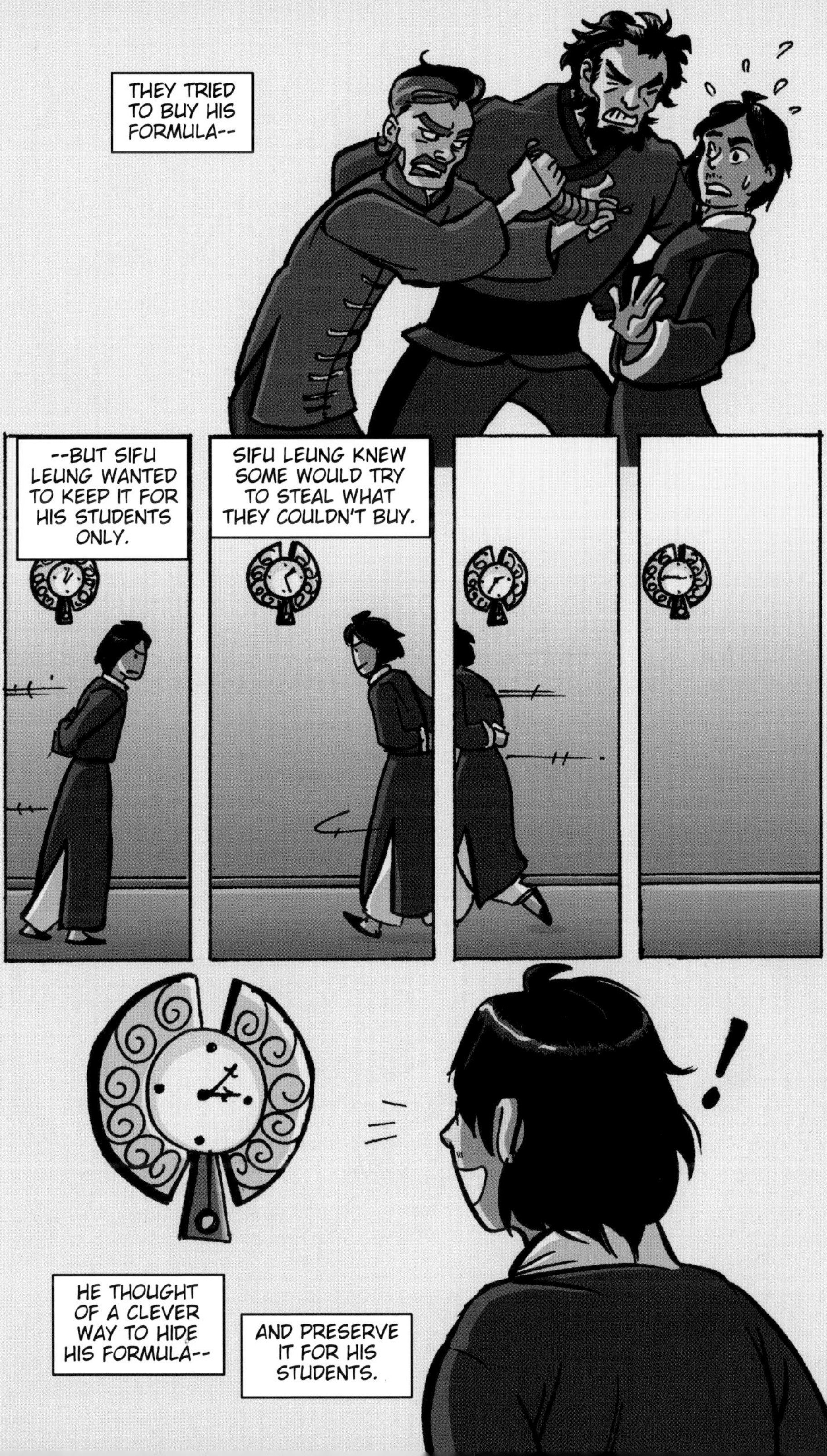
THEY TRIED TO BUY HIS FORMULA--
--BUT SIFU LEUNG WANTED TO KEEP IT FOR HIS STUDENTS ONLY.
SIFU LEUNG KNEW SOME WOULD TRY TO STEAL WHAT THEY COULDN'T BUY.
HE THOUGHT OF A CLEVER WAY TO HIDE HIS FORMULA--
AND PRESERVE IT FOR HIS STUDENTS.

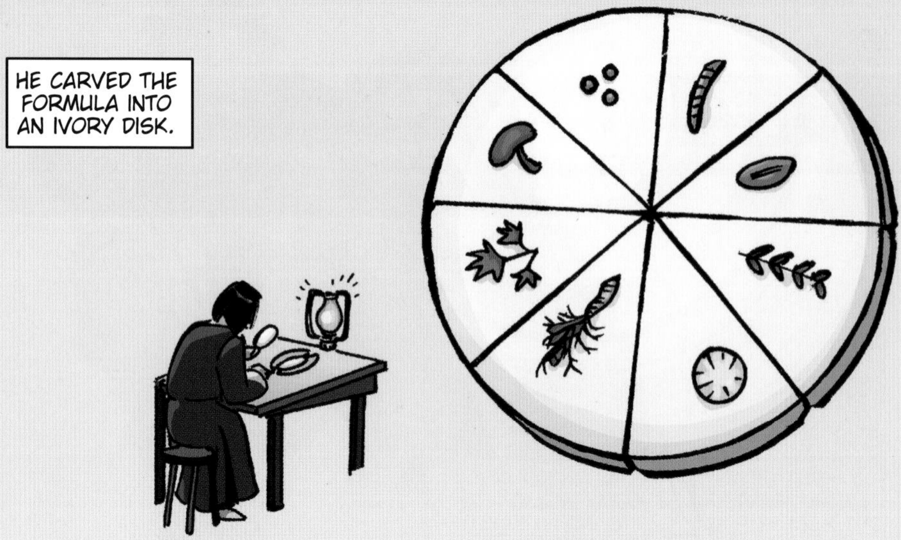
HE CARVED THE FORMULA INTO AN IVORY DISK.

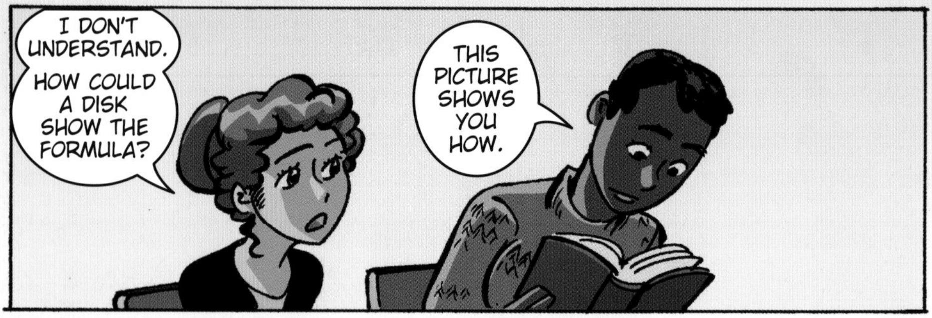
I DON'T UNDERSTAND.
HOW COULD A DISK SHOW THE FORMULA?
THIS PICTURE SHOWS YOU HOW.

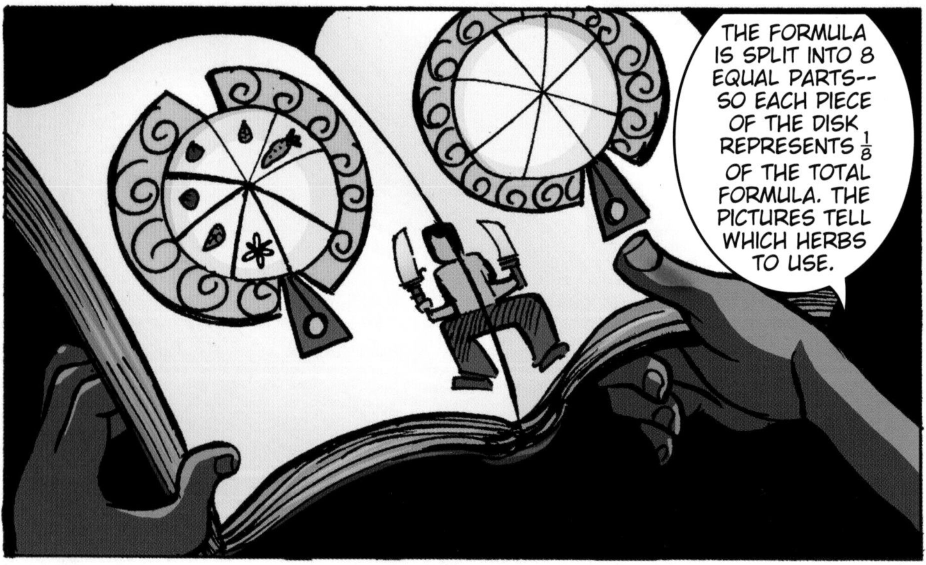
THE FORMULA IS SPLIT INTO 8 EQUAL PARTS-- SO EACH PIECE OF THE DISK REPRESENTS $\frac{1}{8}$ OF THE TOTAL FORMULA. THE PICTURES TELL WHICH HERBS TO USE.

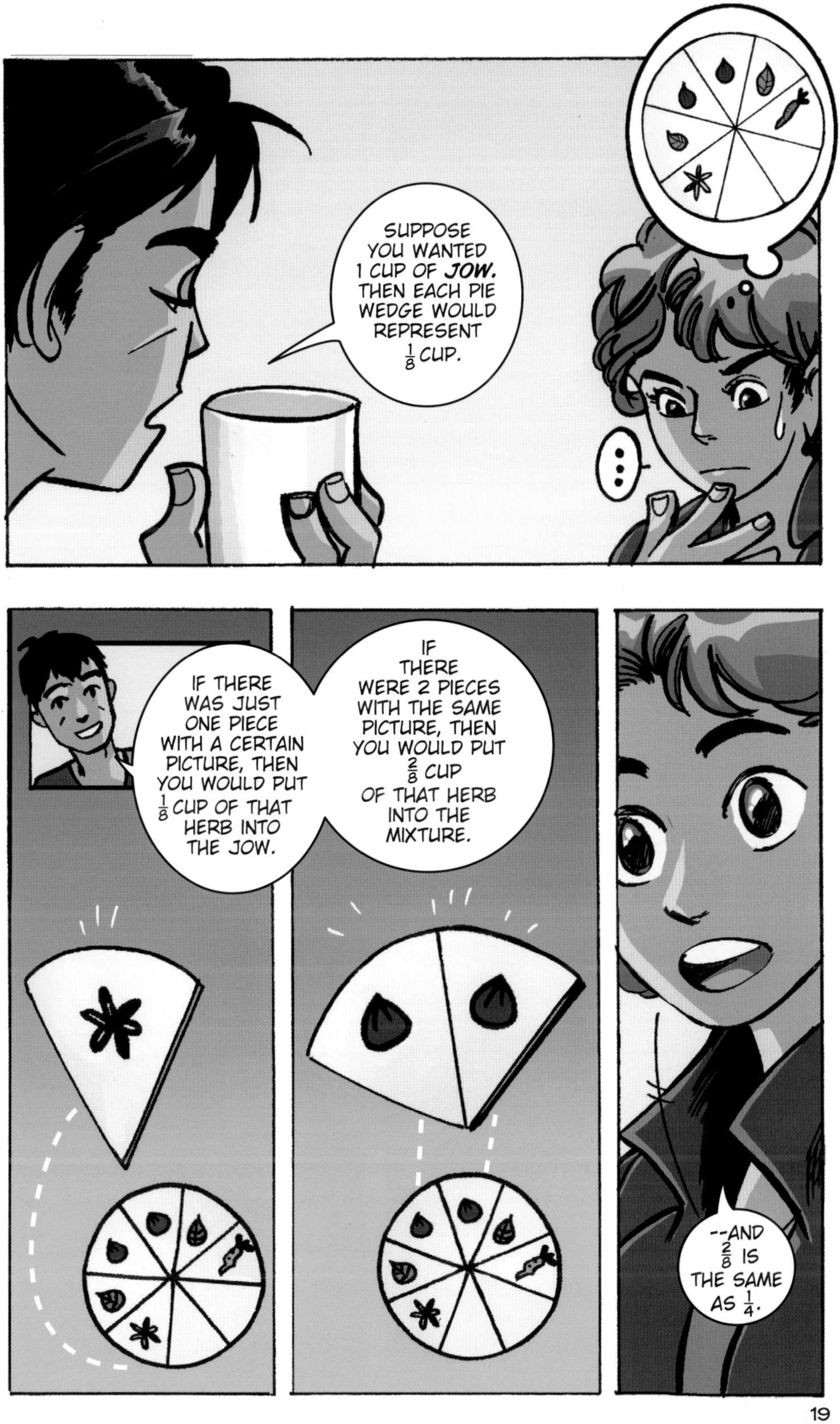
SUPPOSE YOU WANTED 1 CUP OF **JOW.** THEN EACH PIE WEDGE WOULD REPRESENT $\frac{1}{8}$ CUP.
...
IF THERE WAS JUST ONE PIECE WITH A CERTAIN PICTURE, THEN YOU WOULD PUT $\frac{1}{8}$ CUP OF THAT HERB INTO THE JOW.
IF THERE WERE 2 PIECES WITH THE SAME PICTURE, THEN YOU WOULD PUT $\frac{2}{8}$ CUP OF THAT HERB INTO THE MIXTURE.
--AND $\frac{2}{8}$ IS THE SAME AS $\frac{1}{4}$.

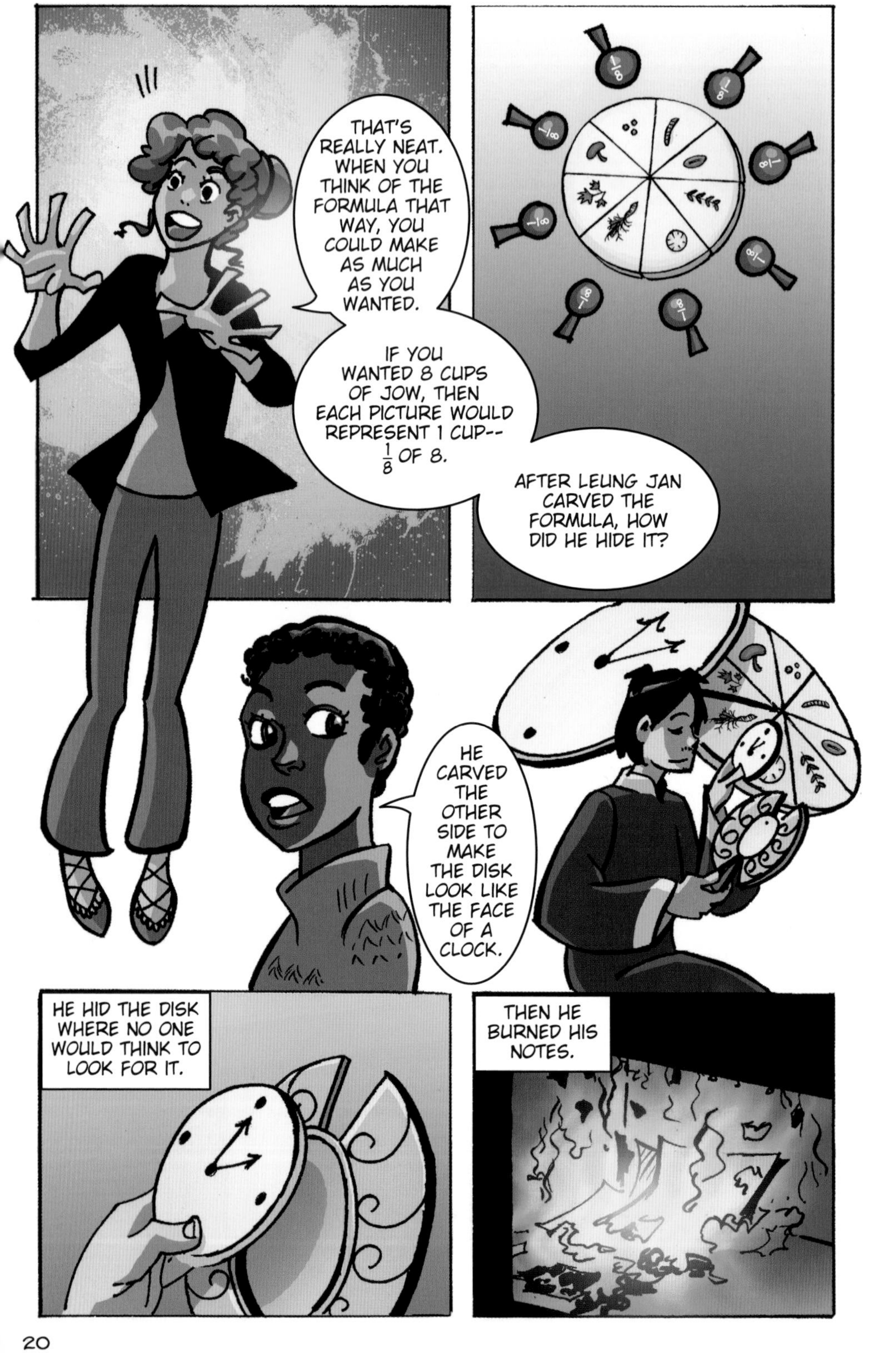

THAT'S REALLY NEAT. WHEN YOU THINK OF THE FORMULA THAT WAY, YOU COULD MAKE AS MUCH AS YOU WANTED.
IF YOU WANTED 8 CUPS OF JOW, THEN EACH PICTURE WOULD REPRESENT 1 CUP-- 1/8 OF 8.
AFTER LEUNG JAN CARVED THE FORMULA, HOW DID HE HIDE IT?
HE CARVED THE OTHER SIDE TO MAKE THE DISK LOOK LIKE THE FACE OF A CLOCK.
HE HID THE DISK WHERE NO ONE WOULD THINK TO LOOK FOR IT.
THEN HE BURNED HIS NOTES.

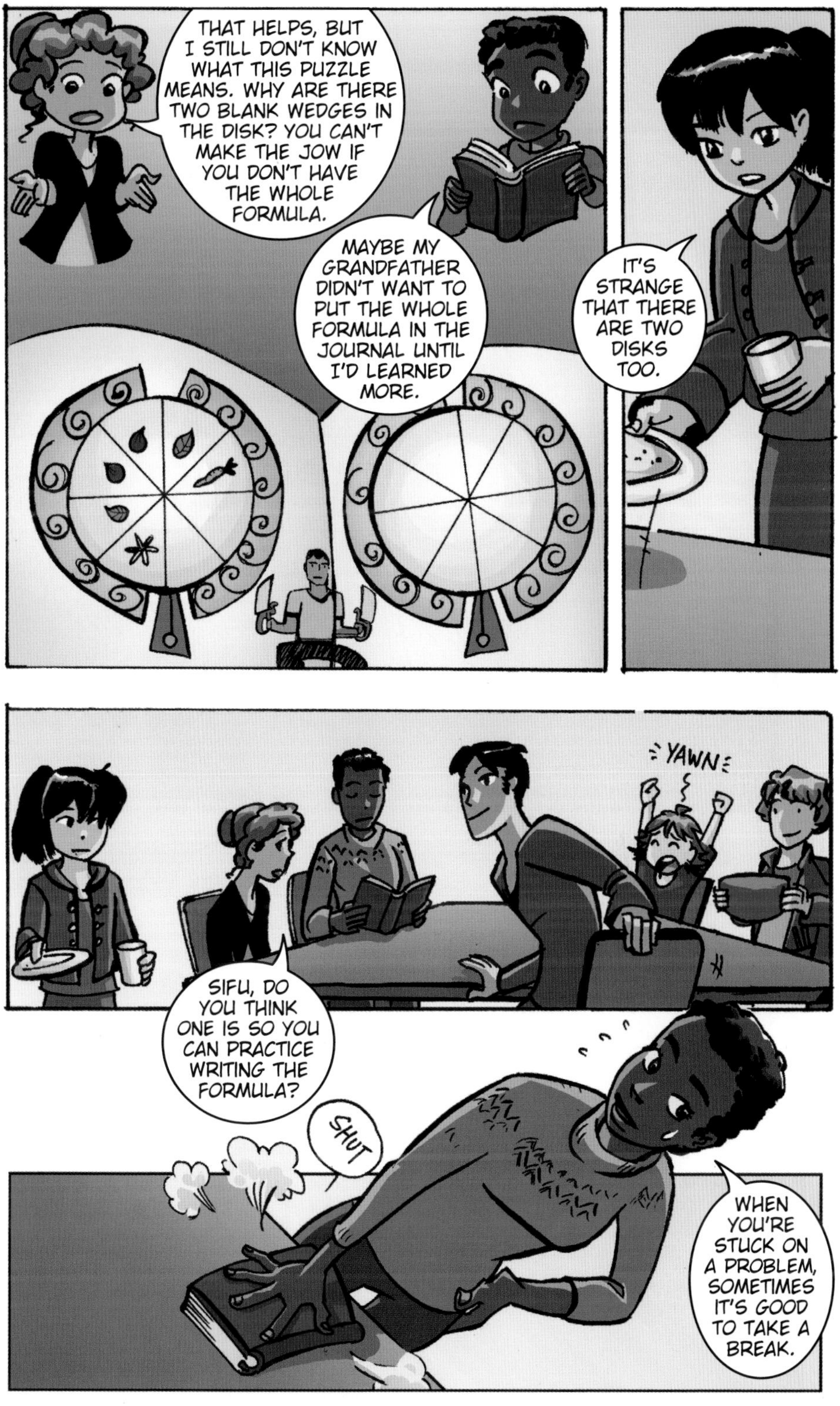
THAT HELPS, BUT I STILL DON'T KNOW WHAT THIS PUZZLE MEANS. WHY ARE THERE TWO BLANK WEDGES IN THE DISK? YOU CAN'T MAKE THE JOW IF YOU DON'T HAVE THE WHOLE FORMULA.
MAYBE MY GRANDFATHER DIDN'T WANT TO PUT THE WHOLE FORMULA IN THE JOURNAL UNTIL I'D LEARNED MORE.
IT'S STRANGE THAT THERE ARE TWO DISKS TOO.
YAWN
SIFU, DO YOU THINK ONE IS SO YOU CAN PRACTICE WRITING THE FORMULA?
SHUT
WHEN YOU'RE STUCK ON A PROBLEM, SOMETIMES IT'S GOOD TO TAKE A BREAK.

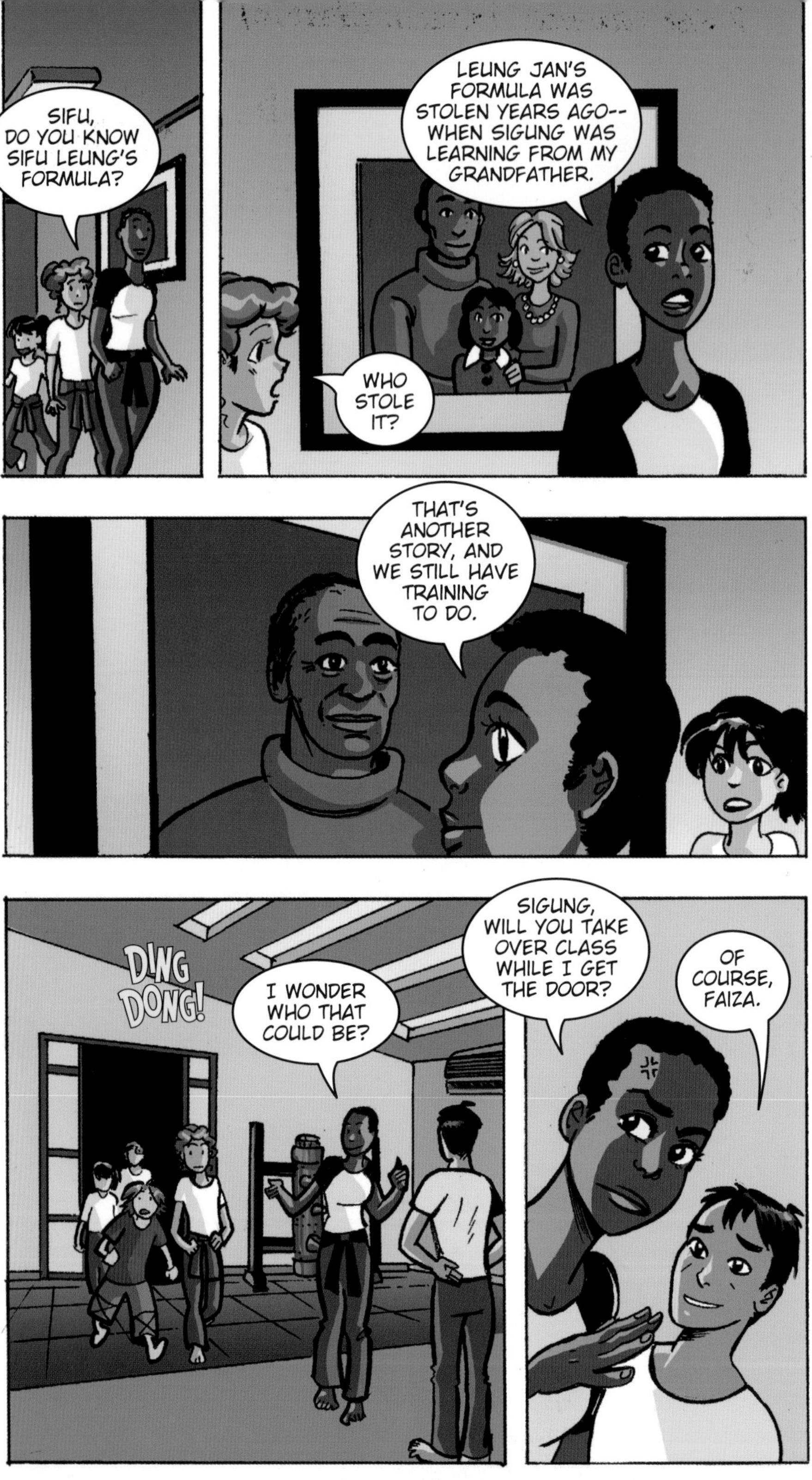
SIFU, DO YOU KNOW SIFU LEUNG'S FORMULA?
LEUNG JAN'S FORMULA WAS STOLEN YEARS AGO-- WHEN SIGUNG WAS LEARNING FROM MY GRANDFATHER.
WHO STOLE IT?
THAT'S ANOTHER STORY, AND WE STILL HAVE TRAINING TO DO.
DING DONG!
I WONDER WHO THAT COULD BE?
SIGUNG, WILL YOU TAKE OVER CLASS WHILE I GET THE DOOR?
OF COURSE, FAIZA.

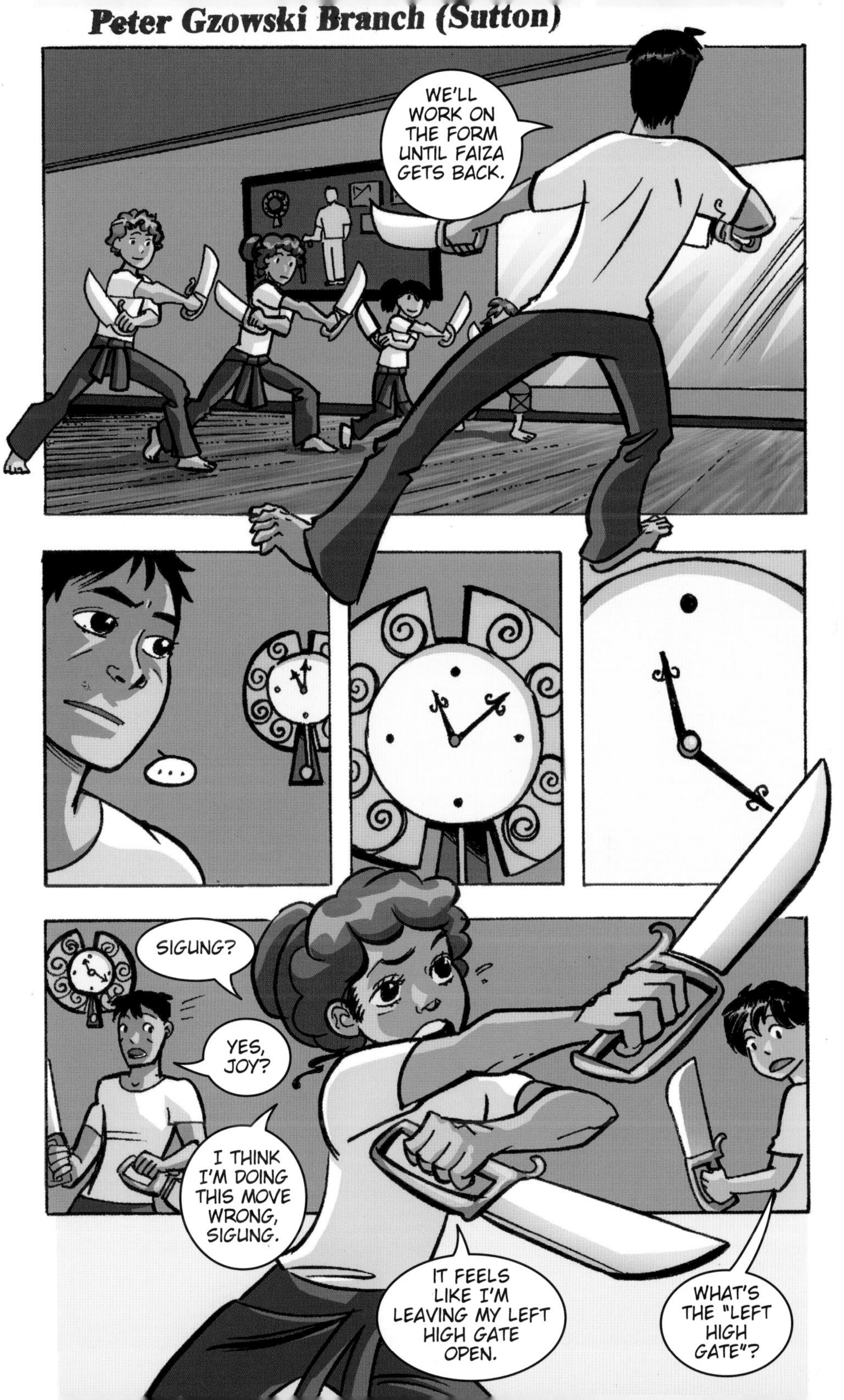
Peter Gzowski Branch (Sutton)
WE'LL WORK ON THE FORM UNTIL FAIZA GETS BACK.
...
SIGUNG?
YES, JOY?
I THINK I'M DOING THIS MOVE WRONG, SIGUNG.
IT FEELS LIKE I'M LEAVING MY LEFT HIGH GATE OPEN.
WHAT'S THE "LEFT HIGH GATE"?

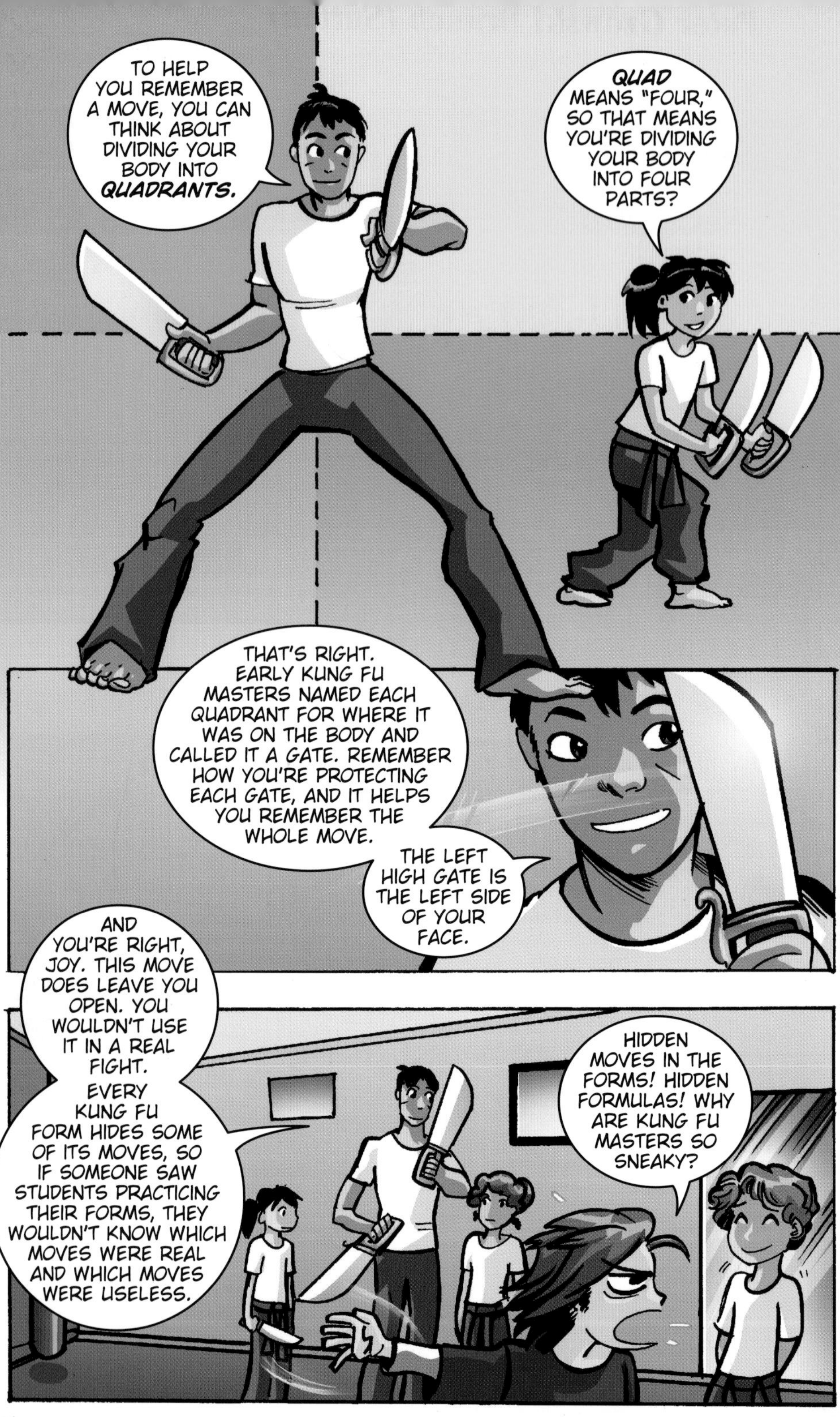
TO HELP YOU REMEMBER A MOVE, YOU CAN THINK ABOUT DIVIDING YOUR BODY INTO QUADRANTS.
QUAD MEANS "FOUR," SO THAT MEANS YOU'RE DIVIDING YOUR BODY INTO FOUR PARTS?
THAT'S RIGHT. EARLY KUNG FU MASTERS NAMED EACH QUADRANT FOR WHERE IT WAS ON THE BODY AND CALLED IT A GATE. REMEMBER HOW YOU'RE PROTECTING EACH GATE, AND IT HELPS YOU REMEMBER THE WHOLE MOVE.
THE LEFT HIGH GATE IS THE LEFT SIDE OF YOUR FACE.
AND YOU'RE RIGHT, JOY. THIS MOVE DOES LEAVE YOU OPEN. YOU WOULDN'T USE IT IN A REAL FIGHT.
EVERY KUNG FU FORM HIDES SOME OF ITS MOVES, SO IF SOMEONE SAW STUDENTS PRACTICING THEIR FORMS, THEY WOULDN'T KNOW WHICH MOVES WERE REAL AND WHICH MOVES WERE USELESS.
HIDDEN MOVES IN THE FORMS! HIDDEN FORMULAS! WHY ARE KUNG FU MASTERS SO SNEAKY?

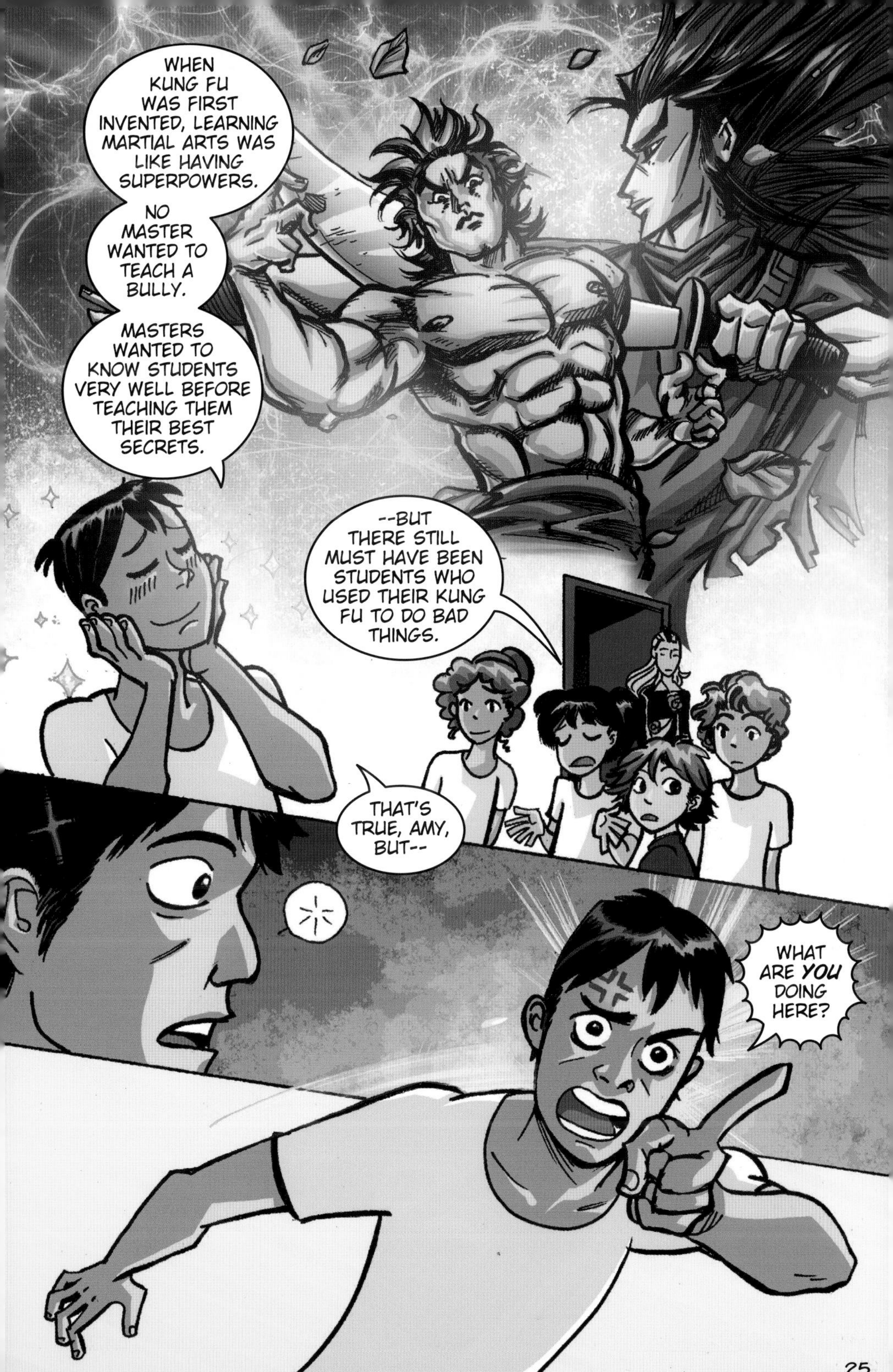
WHEN KUNG FU WAS FIRST INVENTED, LEARNING MARTIAL ARTS WAS LIKE HAVING SUPERPOWERS.
NO MASTER WANTED TO TEACH A BULLY.
MASTERS WANTED TO KNOW STUDENTS VERY WELL BEFORE TEACHING THEM THEIR BEST SECRETS.
--BUT THERE STILL MUST HAVE BEEN STUDENTS WHO USED THEIR KUNG FU TO DO BAD THINGS.
THAT'S TRUE, AMY, BUT--
WHAT ARE *YOU* DOING HERE?

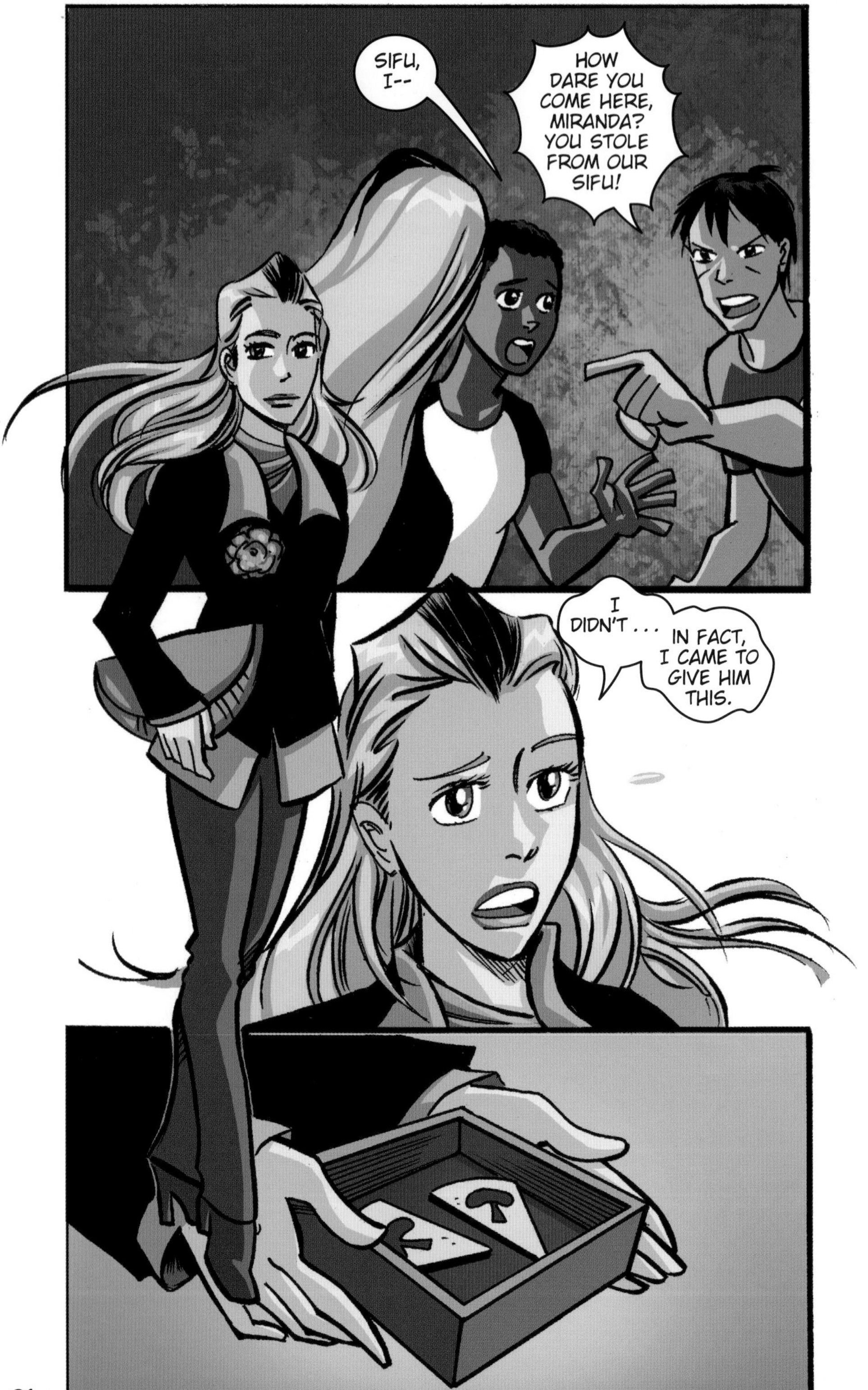
SIFU, I--
HOW DARE YOU COME HERE, MIRANDA? YOU STOLE FROM OUR SIFU!
I DIDN'T . . .
IN FACT, I CAME TO GIVE HIM THIS.

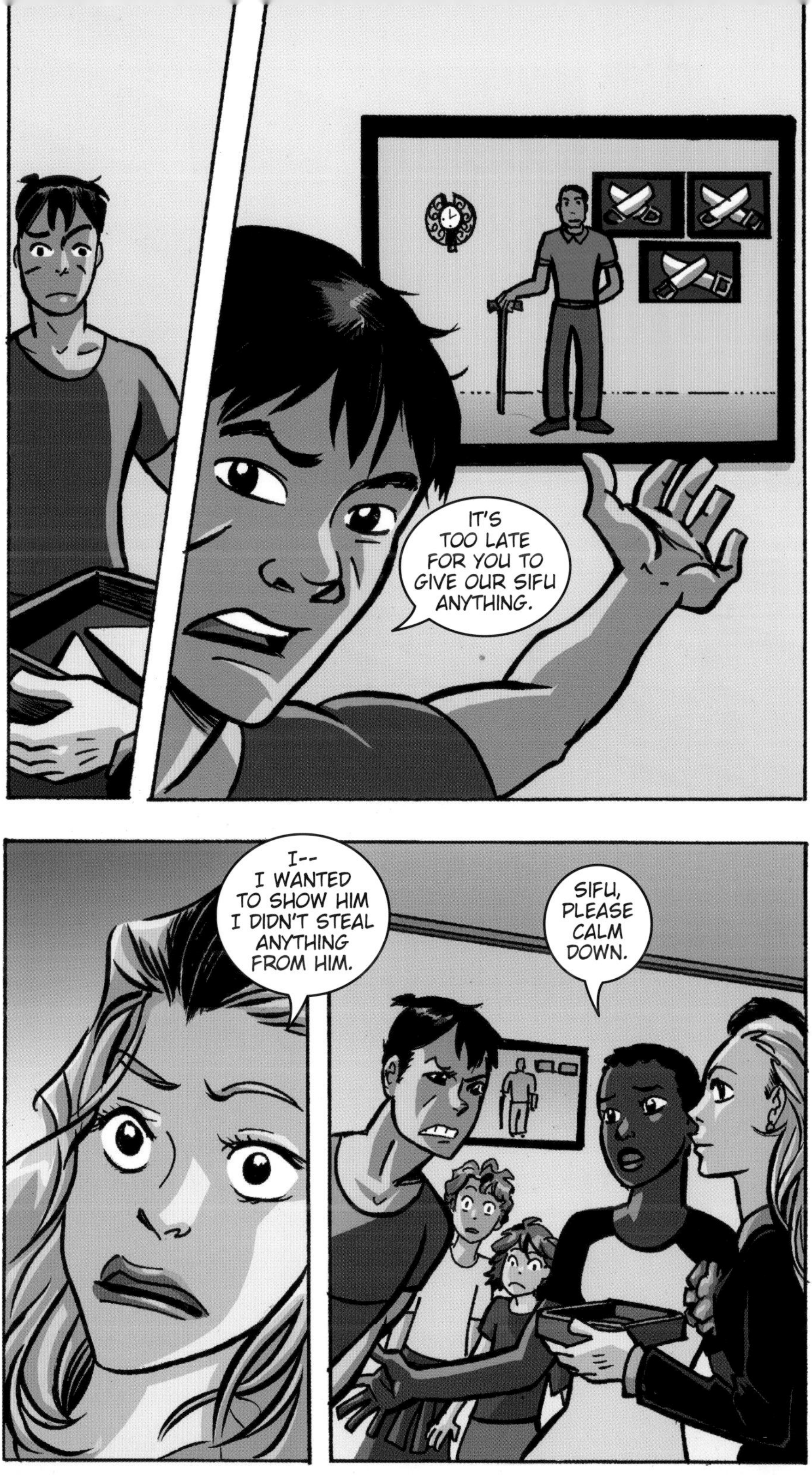
IT'S TOO LATE FOR YOU TO GIVE OUR SIFU ANYTHING.
I-- I WANTED TO SHOW HIM I DIDN'T STEAL ANYTHING FROM HIM.
SIFU, PLEASE CALM DOWN.

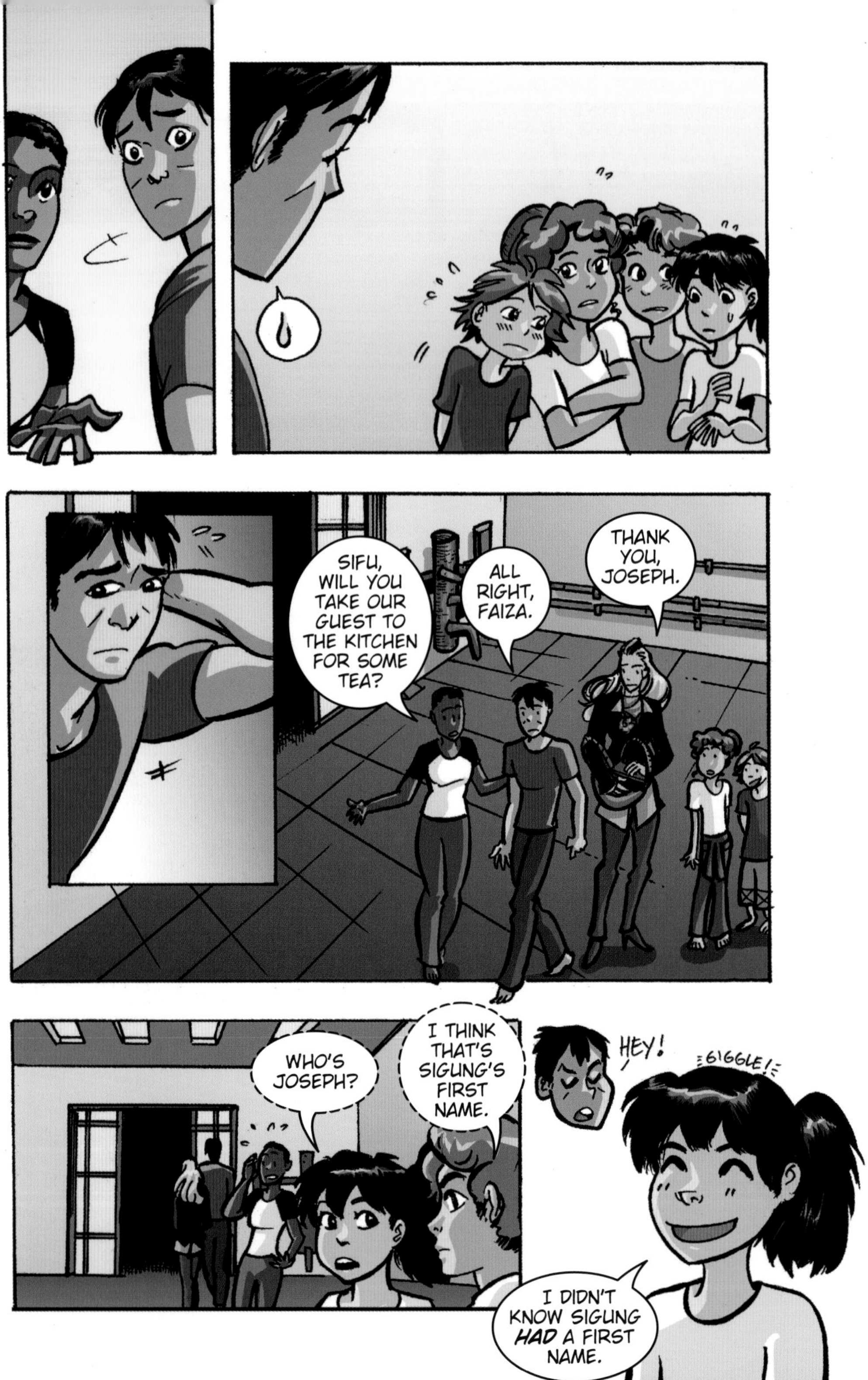
SIFU, WILL YOU TAKE OUR GUEST TO THE KITCHEN FOR SOME TEA?
ALL RIGHT, FAIZA.
THANK YOU, JOSEPH.
WHO'S JOSEPH?
I THINK THAT'S SIGUNG'S FIRST NAME.
HEY!
GIGGLE!
I DIDN'T KNOW SIGUNG HAD A FIRST NAME.

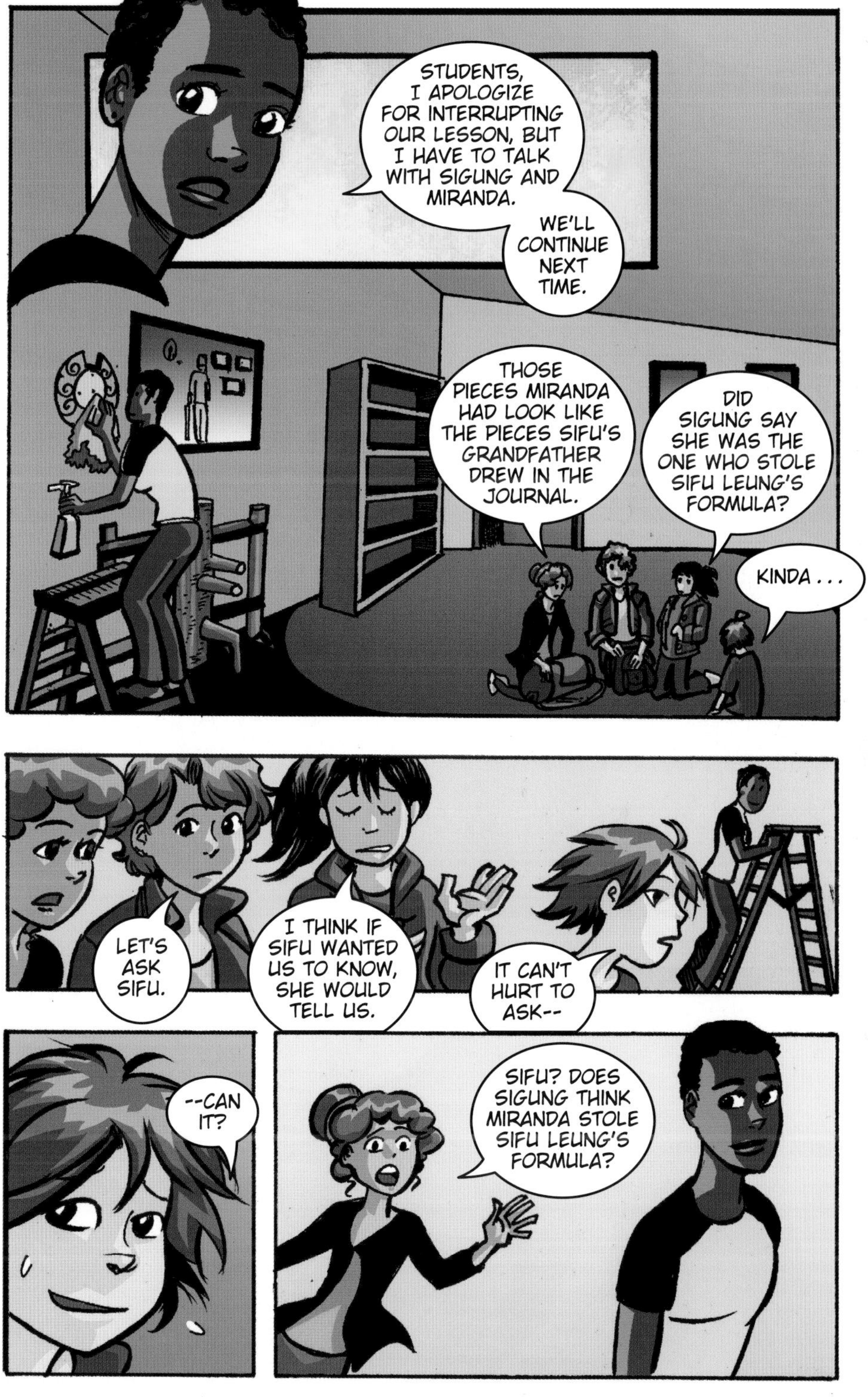
STUDENTS, I APOLOGIZE FOR INTERRUPTING OUR LESSON, BUT I HAVE TO TALK WITH SIGUNG AND MIRANDA.
WE'LL CONTINUE NEXT TIME.
THOSE PIECES MIRANDA HAD LOOK LIKE THE PIECES SIFU'S GRANDFATHER DREW IN THE JOURNAL.
DID SIGUNG SAY SHE WAS THE ONE WHO STOLE SIFU LEUNG'S FORMULA?
KINDA . . .
LET'S ASK SIFU.
I THINK IF SIFU WANTED US TO KNOW, SHE WOULD TELL US.
IT CAN'T HURT TO ASK--
--CAN IT?
SIFU? DOES SIGUNG THINK MIRANDA STOLE SIFU LEUNG'S FORMULA?

YOU DON'T HAVE TO TELL US. MAYBE WE SHOULDN'T HAVE ASKED.

IT'S JUST THAT SIGUNG WAS SO ANGRY, AND WE HEARD MIRANDA SAY SHE DIDN'T STEAL--

WE WEREN'T TRYING TO OVERHEAR, BUT--

--BUT SIGUNG WAS ANGRY, AND HE ACCUSED MIRANDA WHERE YOU COULD HEAR HIM.

YEAH.

ADULTS-- EVEN KUNG FU MASTERS-- AREN'T ALWAYS PERFECT.

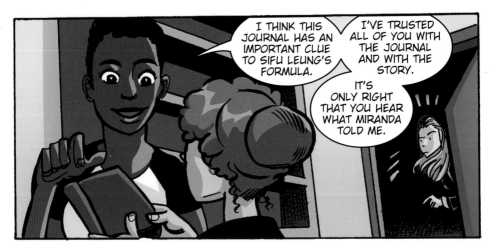

I THINK THIS JOURNAL HAS AN IMPORTANT CLUE TO SIFU LEUNG'S FORMULA.

I'VE TRUSTED ALL OF YOU WITH THE JOURNAL AND WITH THE STORY.

IT'S ONLY RIGHT THAT YOU HEAR WHAT MIRANDA TOLD ME.

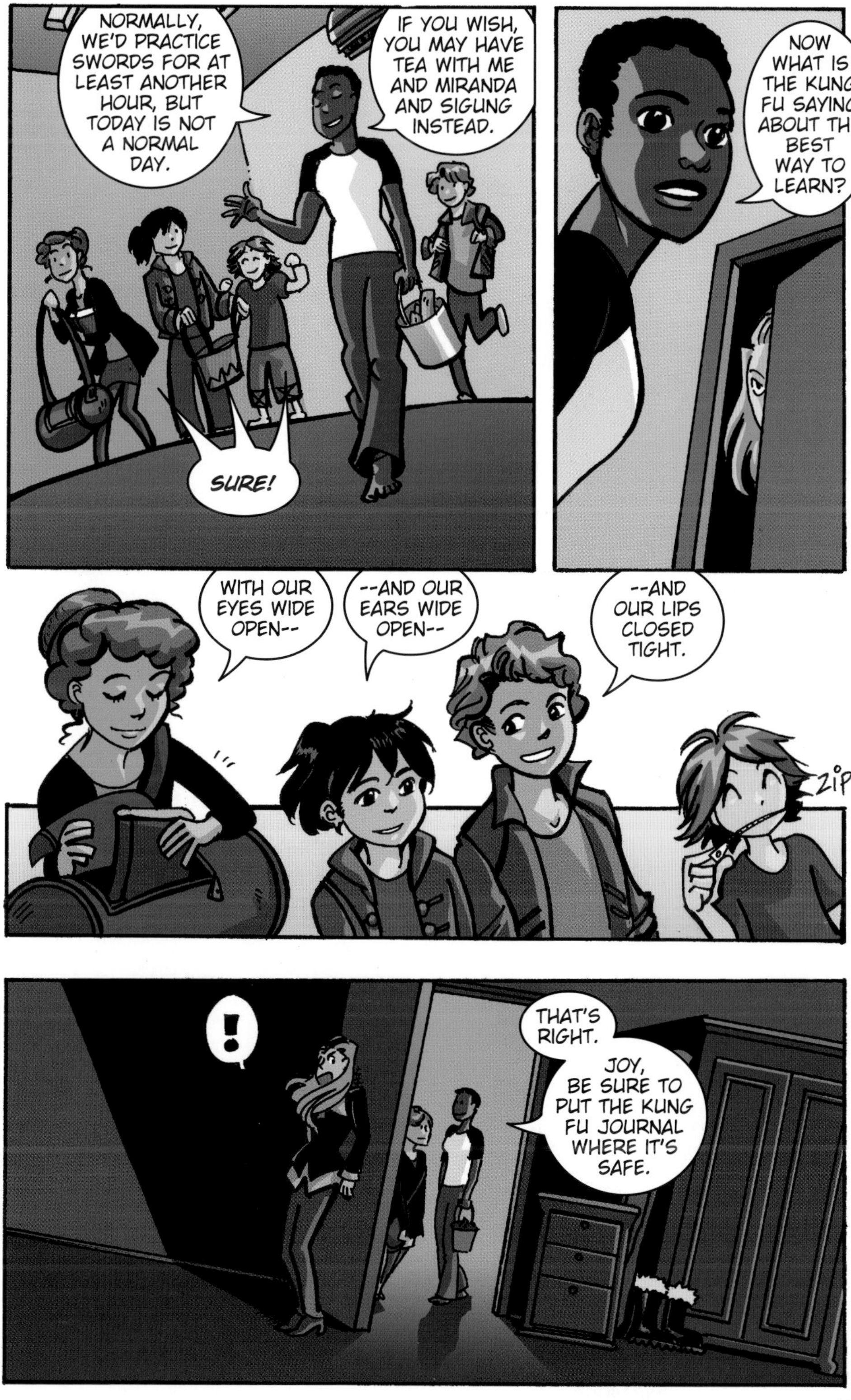
NORMALLY, WE'D PRACTICE SWORDS FOR AT LEAST ANOTHER HOUR, BUT TODAY IS NOT A NORMAL DAY.
IF YOU WISH, YOU MAY HAVE TEA WITH ME AND MIRANDA AND SIGUNG INSTEAD.
SURE!
NOW WHAT IS THE KUNG FU SAYING ABOUT THE BEST WAY TO LEARN?
WITH OUR EYES WIDE OPEN--
--AND OUR EARS WIDE OPEN--
--AND OUR LIPS CLOSED TIGHT.
ZIP!
!
THAT'S RIGHT.
JOY, BE SURE TO PUT THE KUNG FU JOURNAL WHERE IT'S SAFE.

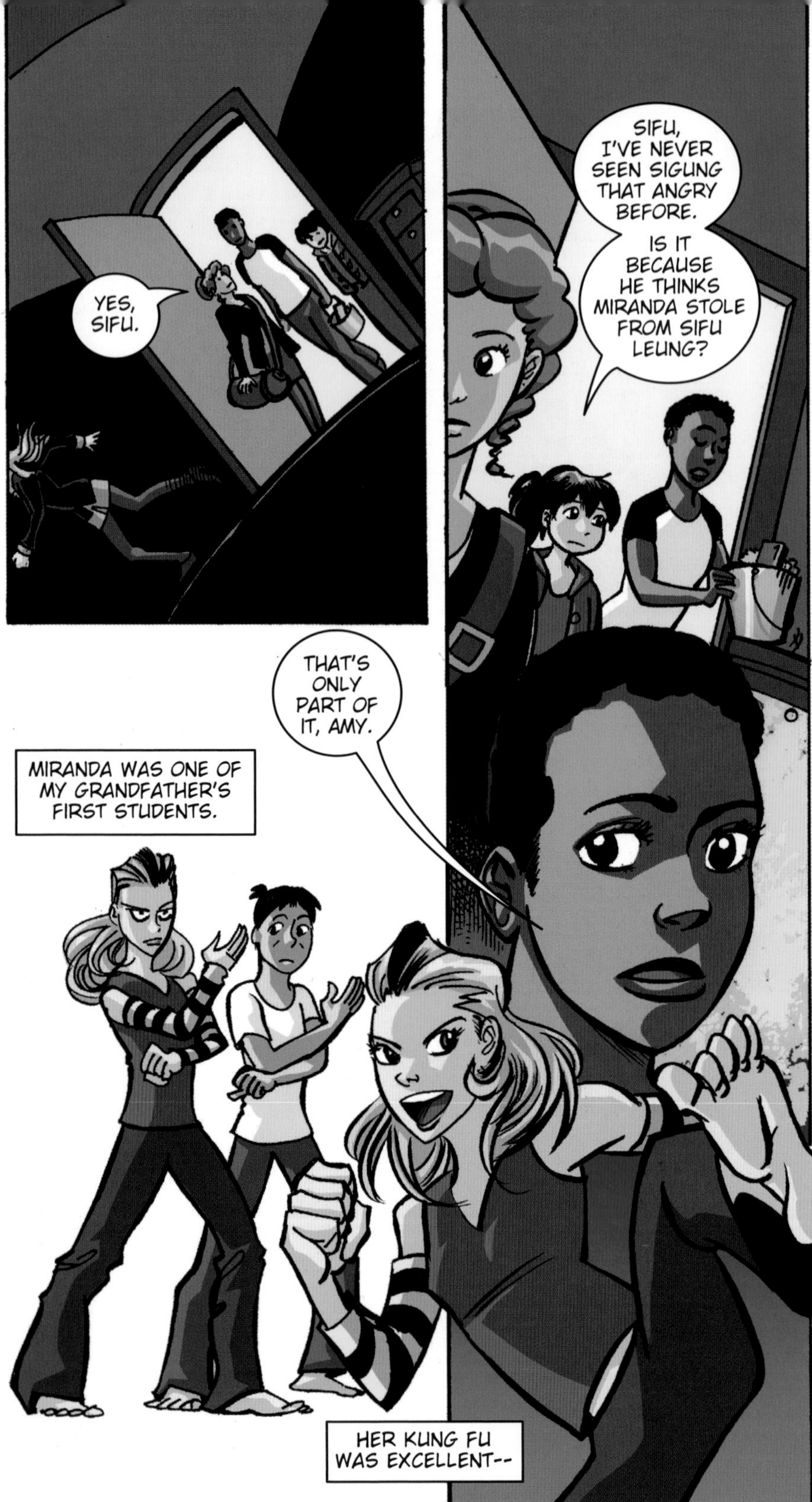
YES, SIFU.
SIFU, I'VE NEVER SEEN SIGUNG THAT ANGRY BEFORE.
IS IT BECAUSE HE THINKS MIRANDA STOLE FROM SIFU LEUNG?
THAT'S ONLY PART OF IT, AMY.
MIRANDA WAS ONE OF MY GRANDFATHER'S FIRST STUDENTS.
HER KUNG FU WAS EXCELLENT--

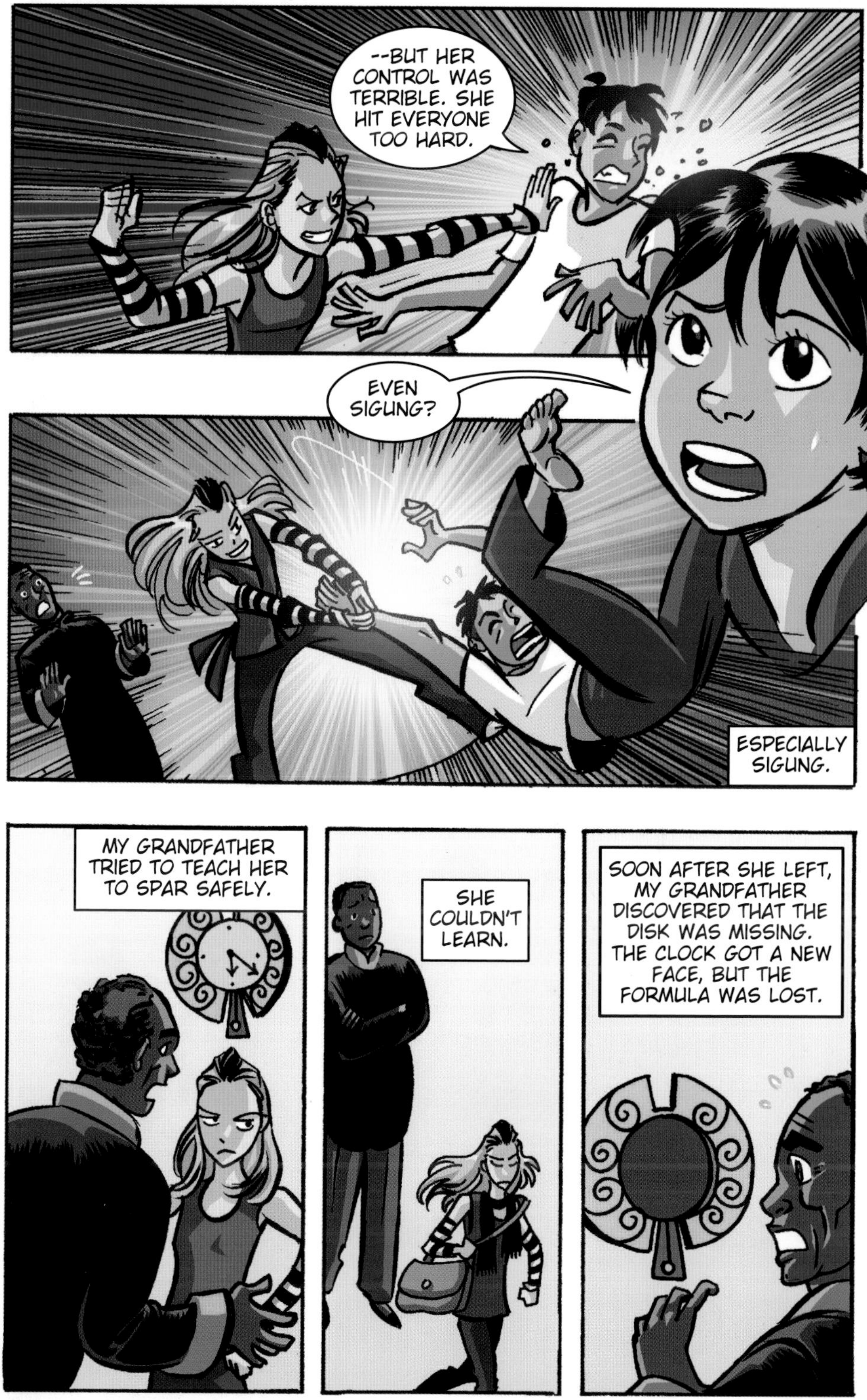
--BUT HER CONTROL WAS TERRIBLE. SHE HIT EVERYONE TOO HARD.
EVEN SIGUNG?
ESPECIALLY SIGUNG.
MY GRANDFATHER TRIED TO TEACH HER TO SPAR SAFELY.
SHE COULDN'T LEARN.
SOON AFTER SHE LEFT, MY GRANDFATHER DISCOVERED THAT THE DISK WAS MISSING. THE CLOCK GOT A NEW FACE, BUT THE FORMULA WAS LOST.

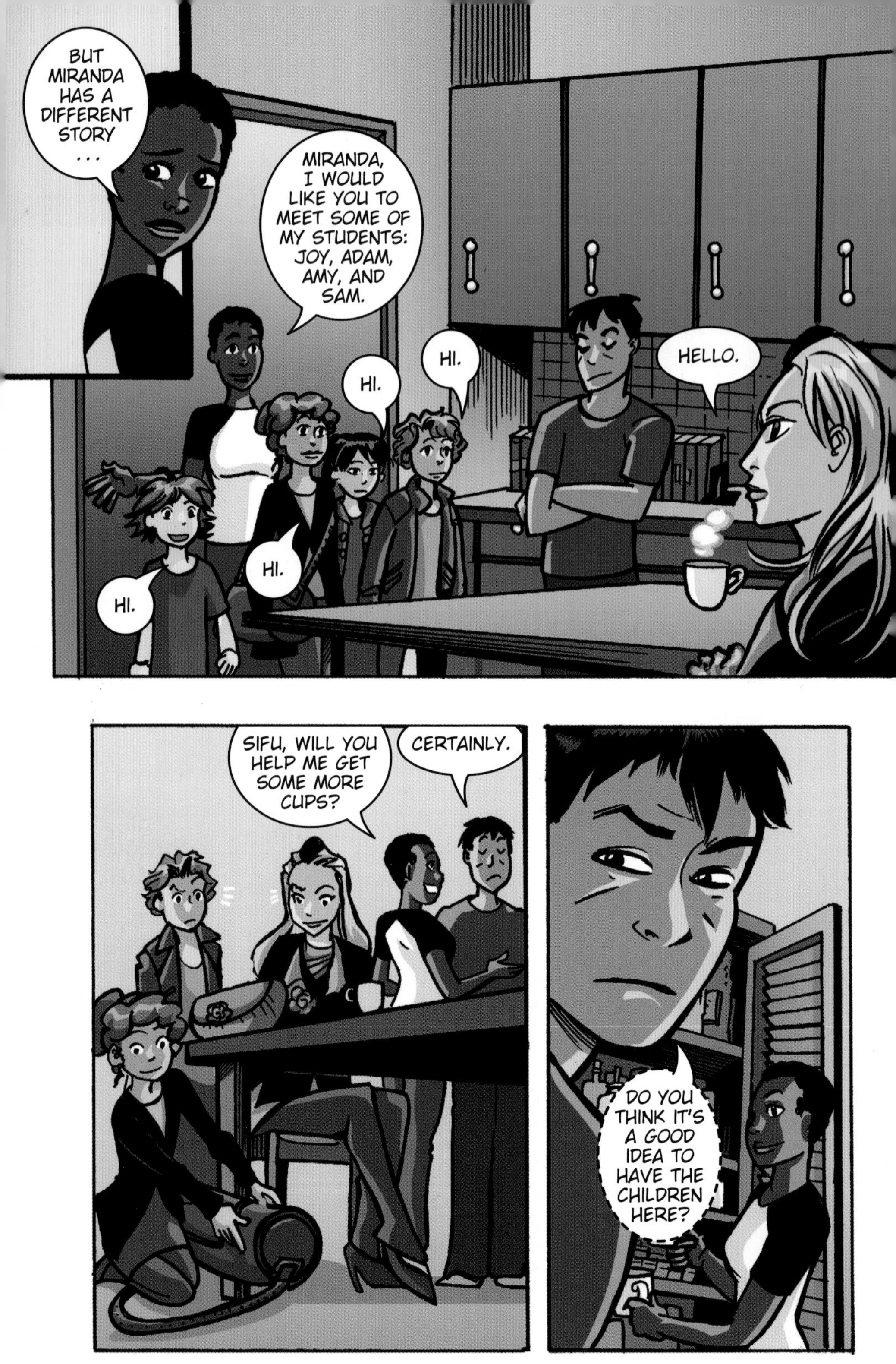
BUT MIRANDA HAS A DIFFERENT STORY . . .
MIRANDA, I WOULD LIKE YOU TO MEET SOME OF MY STUDENTS: JOY, ADAM, AMY, AND SAM.
HI.
HI.
HI.
HI.
HELLO.
SIFU, WILL YOU HELP ME GET SOME MORE CUPS?
CERTAINLY.
DO YOU THINK IT'S A GOOD IDEA TO HAVE THE CHILDREN HERE?

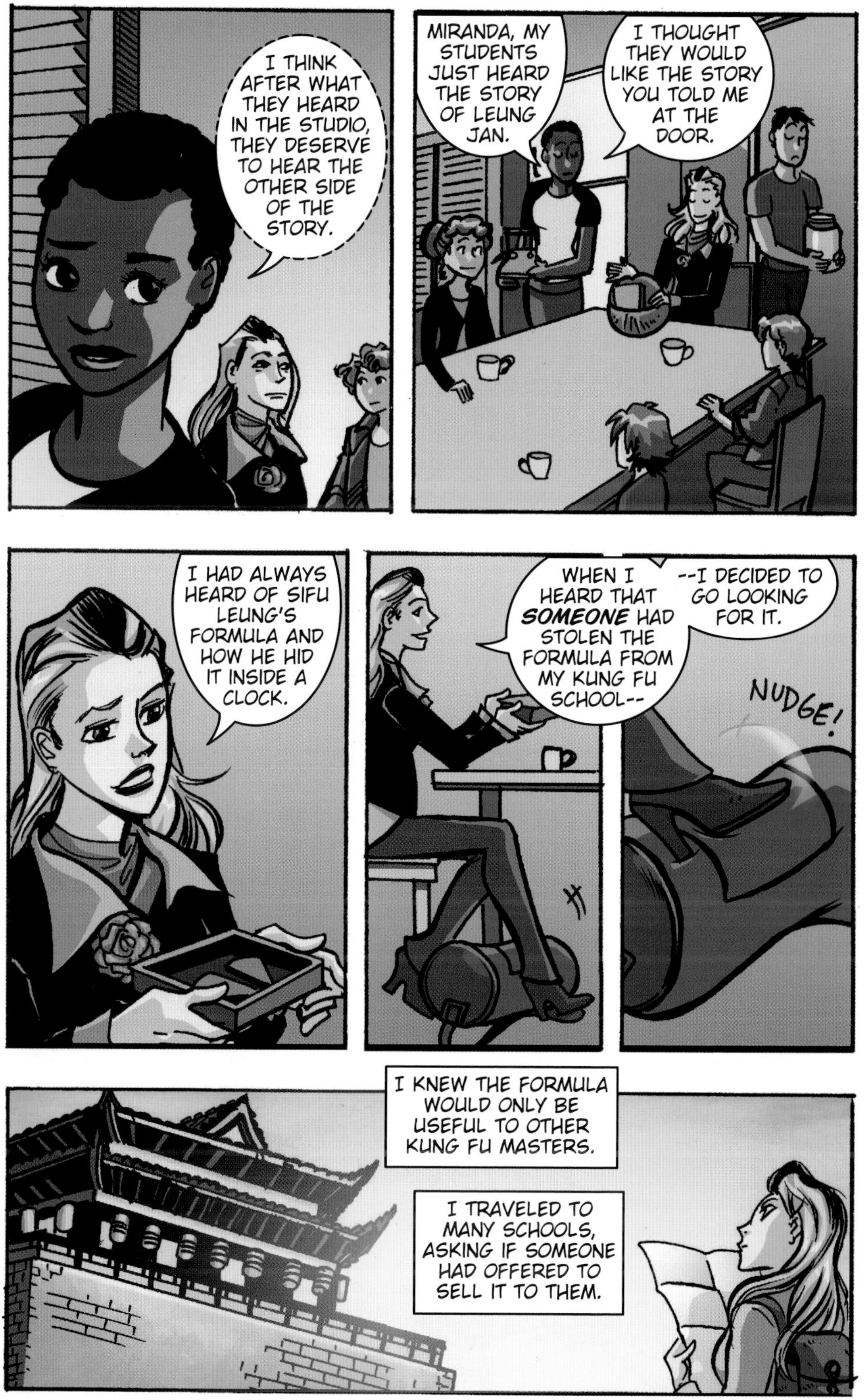
I THINK AFTER WHAT THEY HEARD IN THE STUDIO, THEY DESERVE TO HEAR THE OTHER SIDE OF THE STORY.
MIRANDA, MY STUDENTS JUST HEARD THE STORY OF LEUNG JAN.
I THOUGHT THEY WOULD LIKE THE STORY YOU TOLD ME AT THE DOOR.
I HAD ALWAYS HEARD OF SIFU LEUNG'S FORMULA AND HOW HE HID IT INSIDE A CLOCK.
WHEN I HEARD THAT **SOMEONE** HAD STOLEN THE FORMULA FROM MY KUNG FU SCHOOL--
--I DECIDED TO GO LOOKING FOR IT.
NUDGE!
I KNEW THE FORMULA WOULD ONLY BE USEFUL TO OTHER KUNG FU MASTERS.
I TRAVELED TO MANY SCHOOLS, ASKING IF SOMEONE HAD OFFERED TO SELL IT TO THEM.

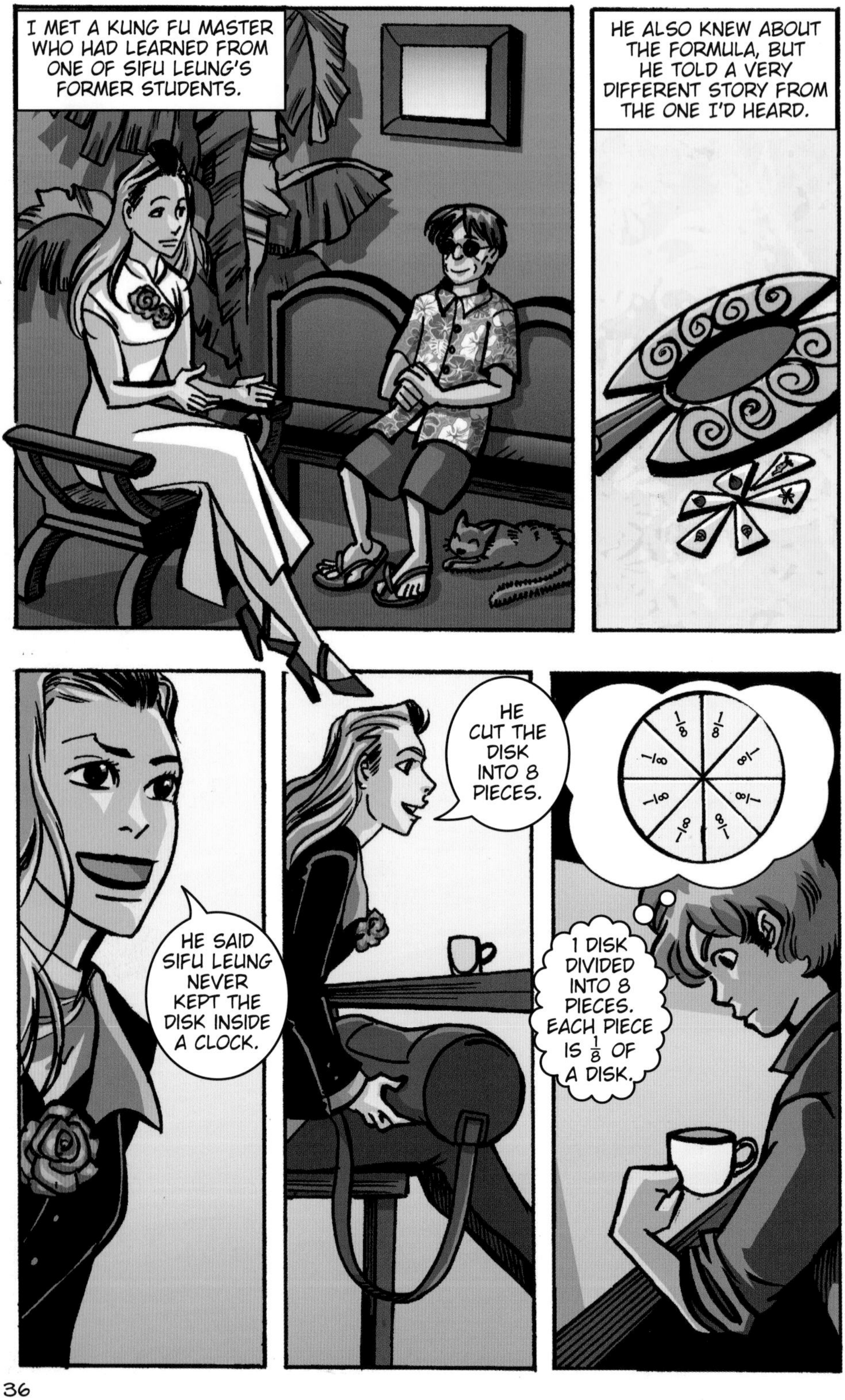
I MET A KUNG FU MASTER WHO HAD LEARNED FROM ONE OF SIFU LEUNG'S FORMER STUDENTS.
HE ALSO KNEW ABOUT THE FORMULA, BUT HE TOLD A VERY DIFFERENT STORY FROM THE ONE I'D HEARD.
HE SAID SIFU LEUNG NEVER KEPT THE DISK INSIDE A CLOCK.
HE CUT THE DISK INTO 8 PIECES.
$\frac{1}{8}$
$\frac{1}{8}$
$\frac{1}{8}$
$\frac{1}{8}$
$\frac{1}{8}$
$\frac{1}{8}$
$\frac{1}{8}$
$\frac{1}{8}$
1 DISK DIVIDED INTO 8 PIECES. EACH PIECE IS $\frac{1}{8}$ OF A DISK.

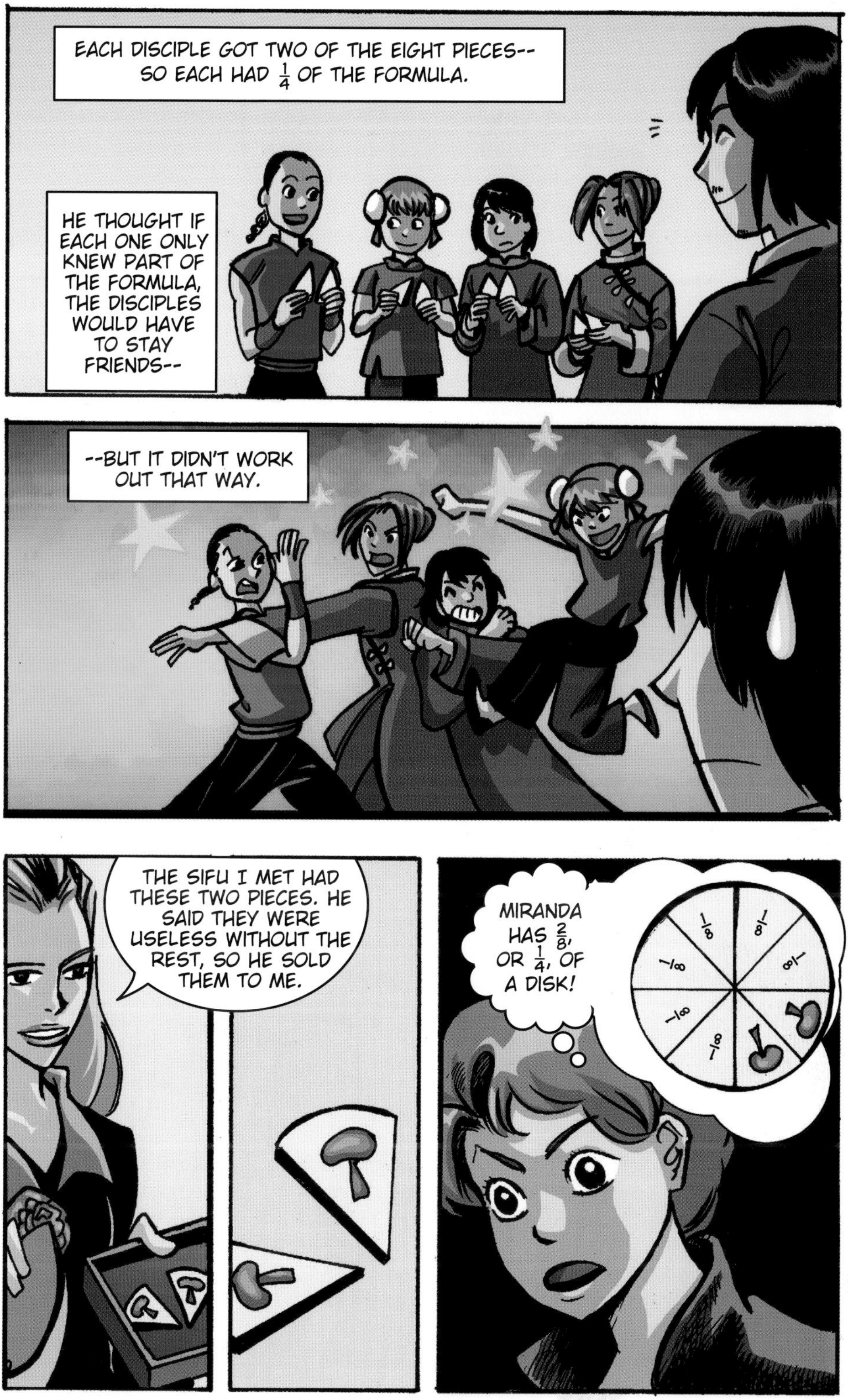
EACH DISCIPLE GOT TWO OF THE EIGHT PIECES-- SO EACH HAD $\frac{1}{4}$ OF THE FORMULA.
HE THOUGHT IF EACH ONE ONLY KNEW PART OF THE FORMULA, THE DISCIPLES WOULD HAVE TO STAY FRIENDS--
--BUT IT DIDN'T WORK OUT THAT WAY.
THE SIFU I MET HAD THESE TWO PIECES. HE SAID THEY WERE USELESS WITHOUT THE REST, SO HE SOLD THEM TO ME.
MIRANDA HAS $\frac{2}{8}$, OR $\frac{1}{4}$, OF A DISK!
$\frac{1}{8}$
$\frac{1}{8}$
$\frac{1}{8}$
$\frac{1}{8}$
$\frac{1}{8}$
$\frac{1}{8}$

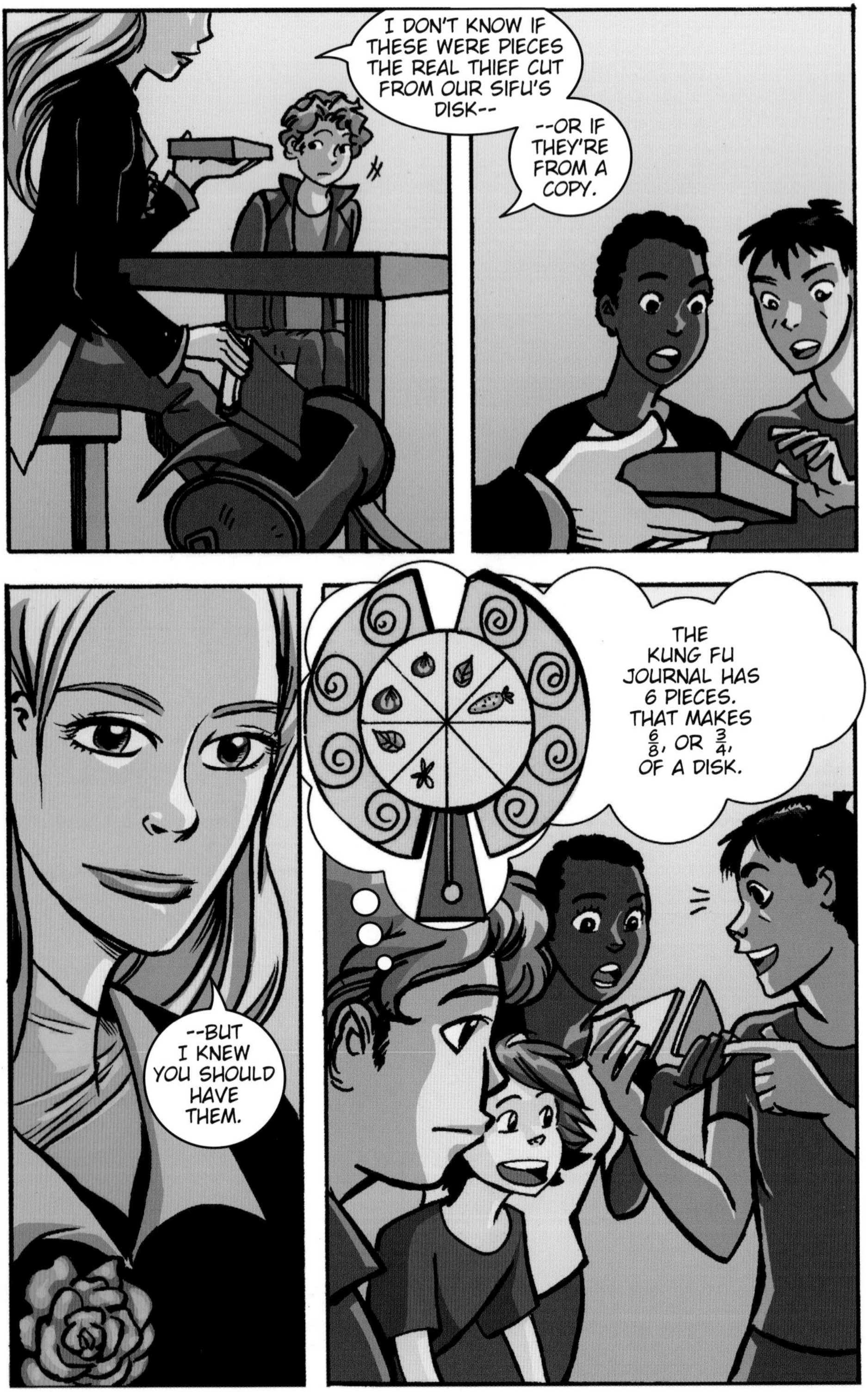
I DON'T KNOW IF THESE WERE PIECES THE REAL THIEF CUT FROM OUR SIFU'S DISK--
--OR IF THEY'RE FROM A COPY.
--BUT I KNEW YOU SHOULD HAVE THEM.
THE KUNG FU JOURNAL HAS 6 PIECES. THAT MAKES $\frac{6}{8}$, OR $\frac{3}{4}$, OF A DISK.

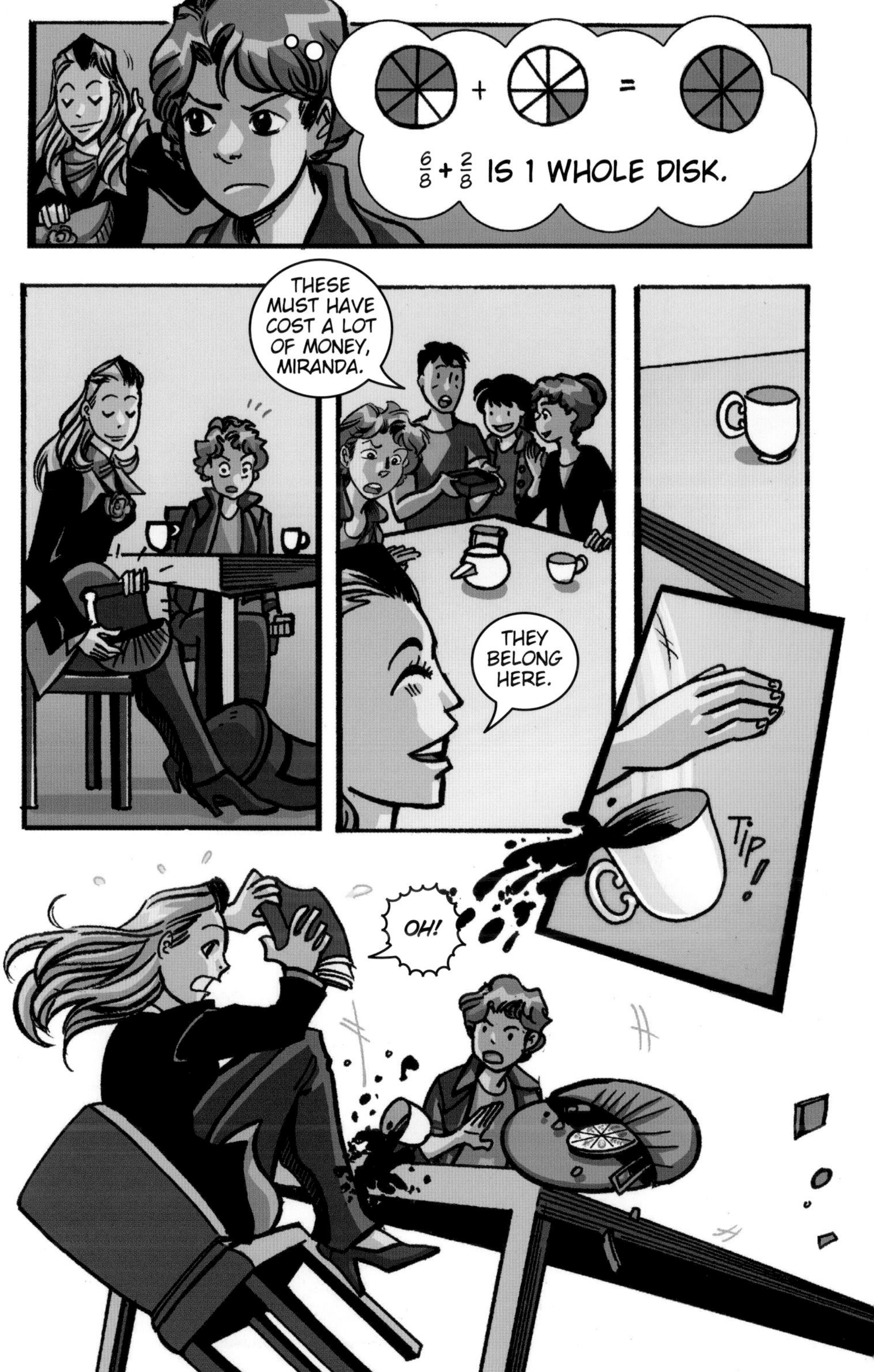
+
=
$\frac{6}{8} + \frac{2}{8}$ IS 1 WHOLE DISK.
THESE MUST HAVE COST A LOT OF MONEY, MIRANDA.
THEY BELONG HERE.
TIP!
OH!

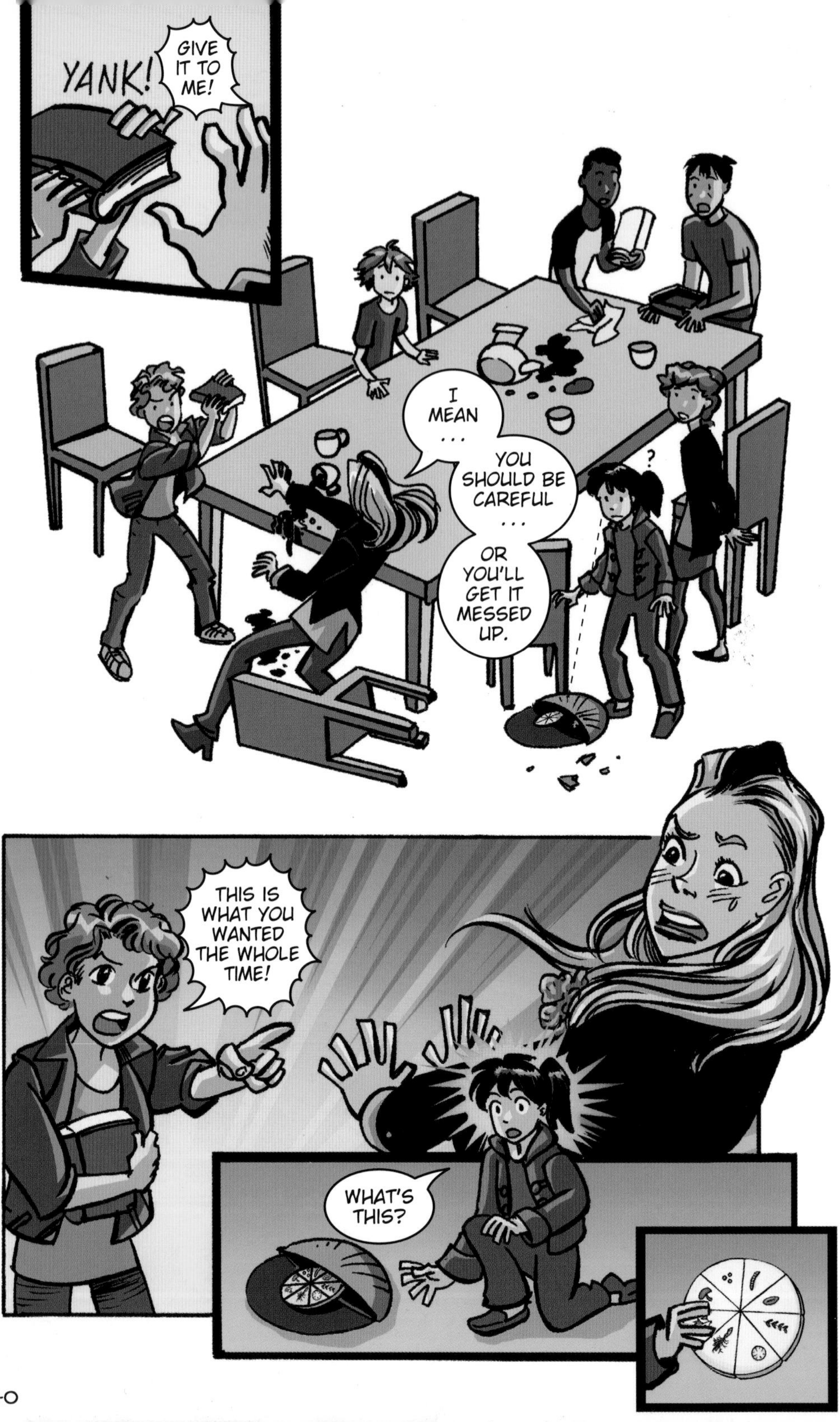
YANK!
GIVE IT TO ME!
I MEAN . . .
YOU SHOULD BE CAREFUL . . .
OR YOU'LL GET IT MESSED UP.
?
THIS IS WHAT YOU WANTED THE WHOLE TIME!
WHAT'S THIS?

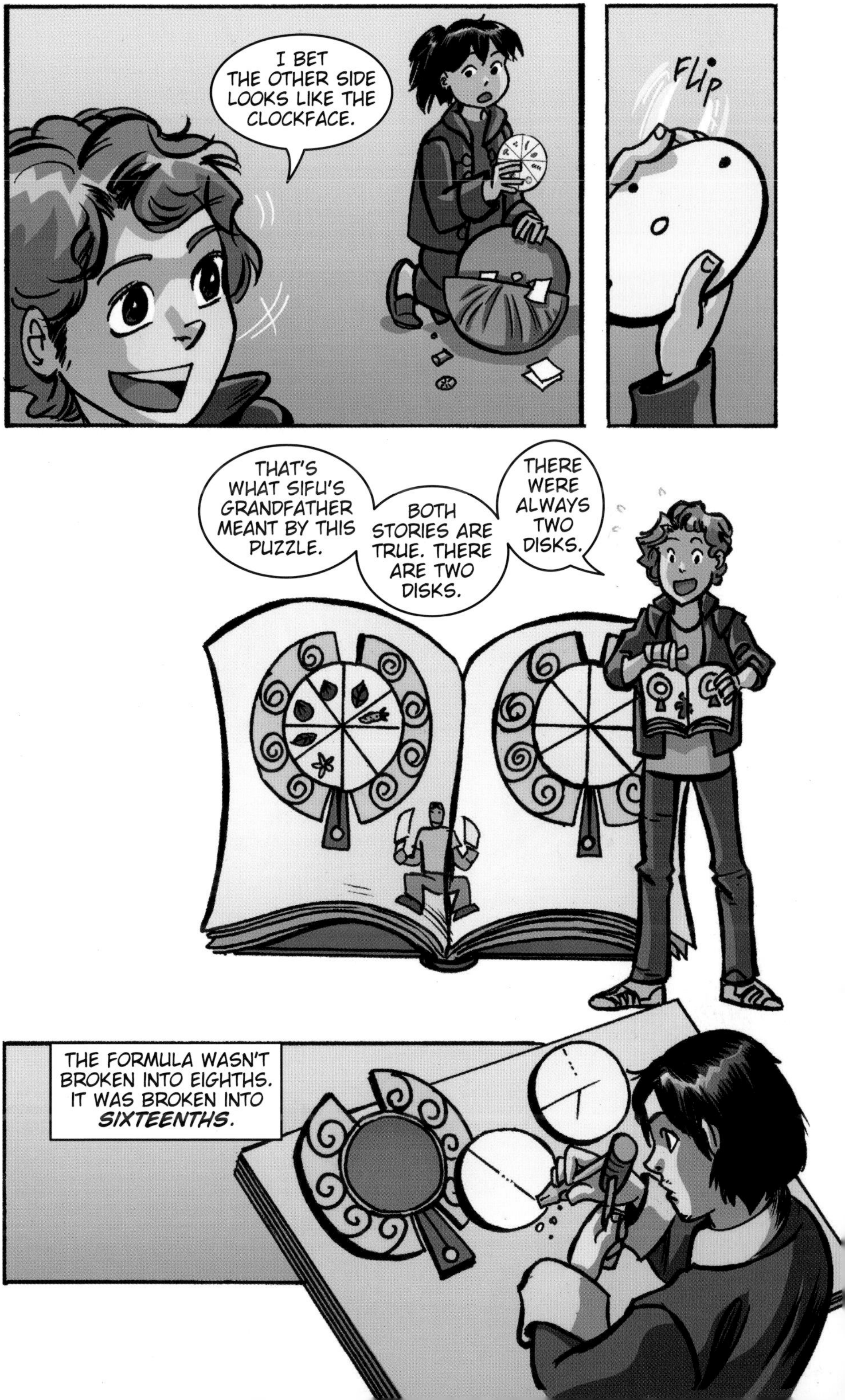
I BET THE OTHER SIDE LOOKS LIKE THE CLOCKFACE.
FLIP
THAT'S WHAT SIFU'S GRANDFATHER MEANT BY THIS PUZZLE.
BOTH STORIES ARE TRUE. THERE ARE TWO DISKS.
THERE WERE ALWAYS TWO DISKS.
THE FORMULA WASN'T BROKEN INTO EIGHTHS. IT WAS BROKEN INTO *SIXTEENTHS*.

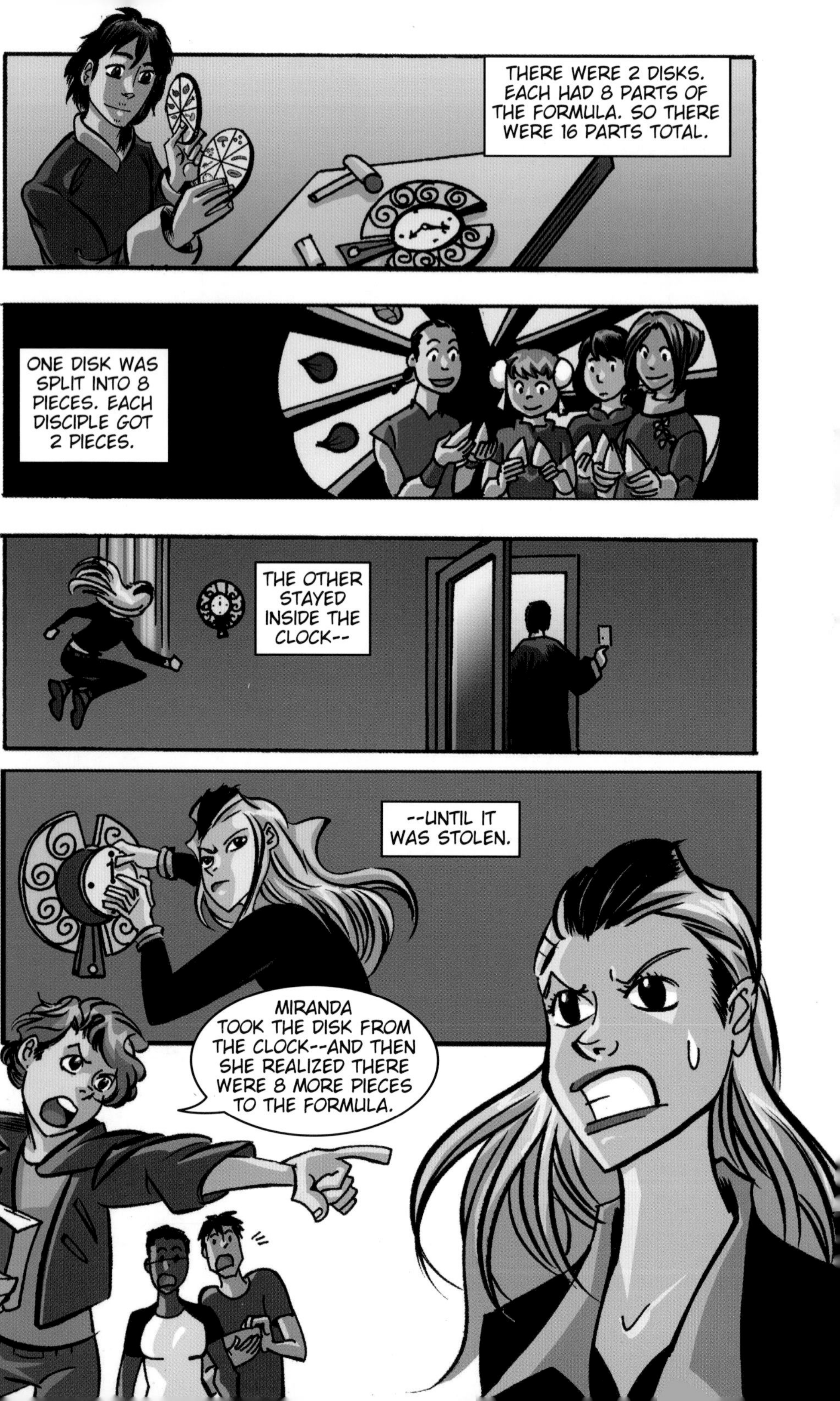
THERE WERE 2 DISKS. EACH HAD 8 PARTS OF THE FORMULA. SO THERE WERE 16 PARTS TOTAL.
ONE DISK WAS SPLIT INTO 8 PIECES. EACH DISCIPLE GOT 2 PIECES.
THE OTHER STAYED INSIDE THE CLOCK--
--UNTIL IT WAS STOLEN.
MIRANDA TOOK THE DISK FROM THE CLOCK--AND THEN SHE REALIZED THERE WERE 8 MORE PIECES TO THE FORMULA.

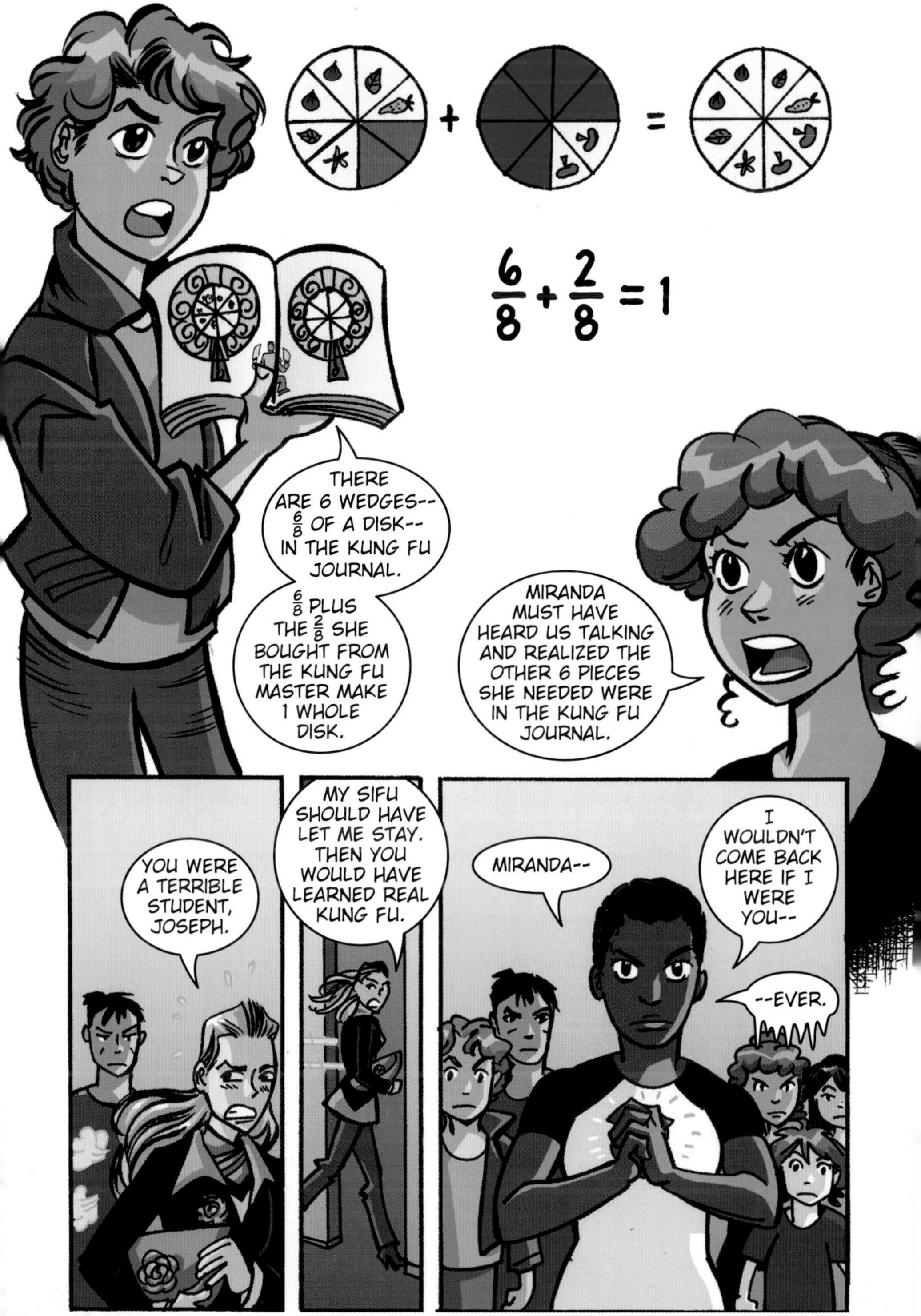

+
=
6/8 + 2/8 = 1
THERE ARE 6 WEDGES-- 6/8 OF A DISK-- IN THE KUNG FU JOURNAL.
6/8 PLUS THE 2/8 SHE BOUGHT FROM THE KUNG FU MASTER MAKE 1 WHOLE DISK.
MIRANDA MUST HAVE HEARD US TALKING AND REALIZED THE OTHER 6 PIECES SHE NEEDED WERE IN THE KUNG FU JOURNAL.
YOU WERE A TERRIBLE STUDENT, JOSEPH.
MY SIFU SHOULD HAVE LET ME STAY. THEN YOU WOULD HAVE LEARNED REAL KUNG FU.
MIRANDA--
I WOULDN'T COME BACK HERE IF I WERE YOU--
--EVER.

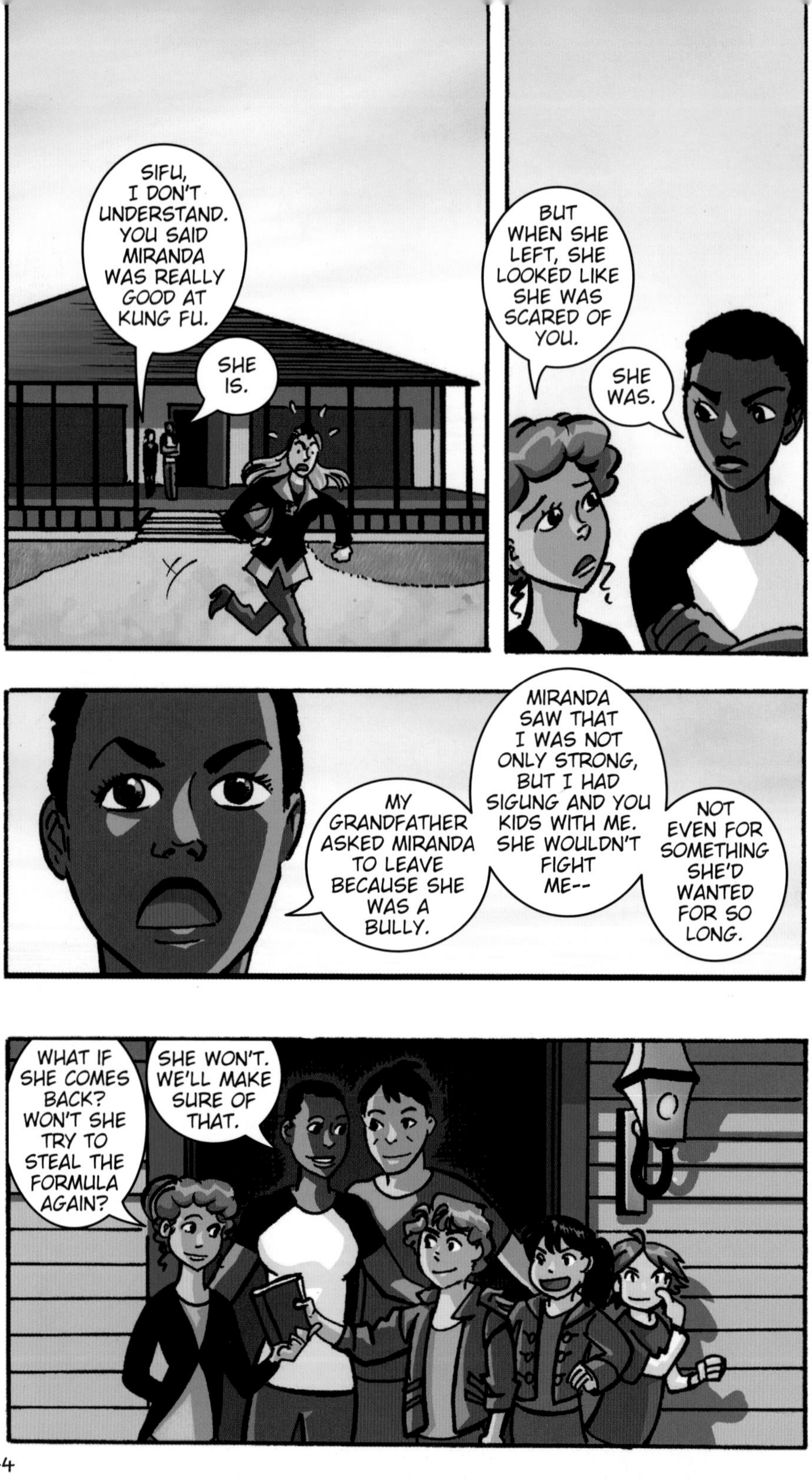
SIFU, I DON'T UNDERSTAND. YOU SAID MIRANDA WAS REALLY GOOD AT KUNG FU.
SHE IS.
BUT WHEN SHE LEFT, SHE LOOKED LIKE SHE WAS SCARED OF YOU.
SHE WAS.
MY GRANDFATHER ASKED MIRANDA TO LEAVE BECAUSE SHE WAS A BULLY.
MIRANDA SAW THAT I WAS NOT ONLY STRONG, BUT I HAD SIGUNG AND YOU KIDS WITH ME. SHE WOULDN'T FIGHT ME--
NOT EVEN FOR SOMETHING SHE'D WANTED FOR SO LONG.
WHAT IF SHE COMES BACK? WON'T SHE TRY TO STEAL THE FORMULA AGAIN?
SHE WON'T. WE'LL MAKE SURE OF THAT.

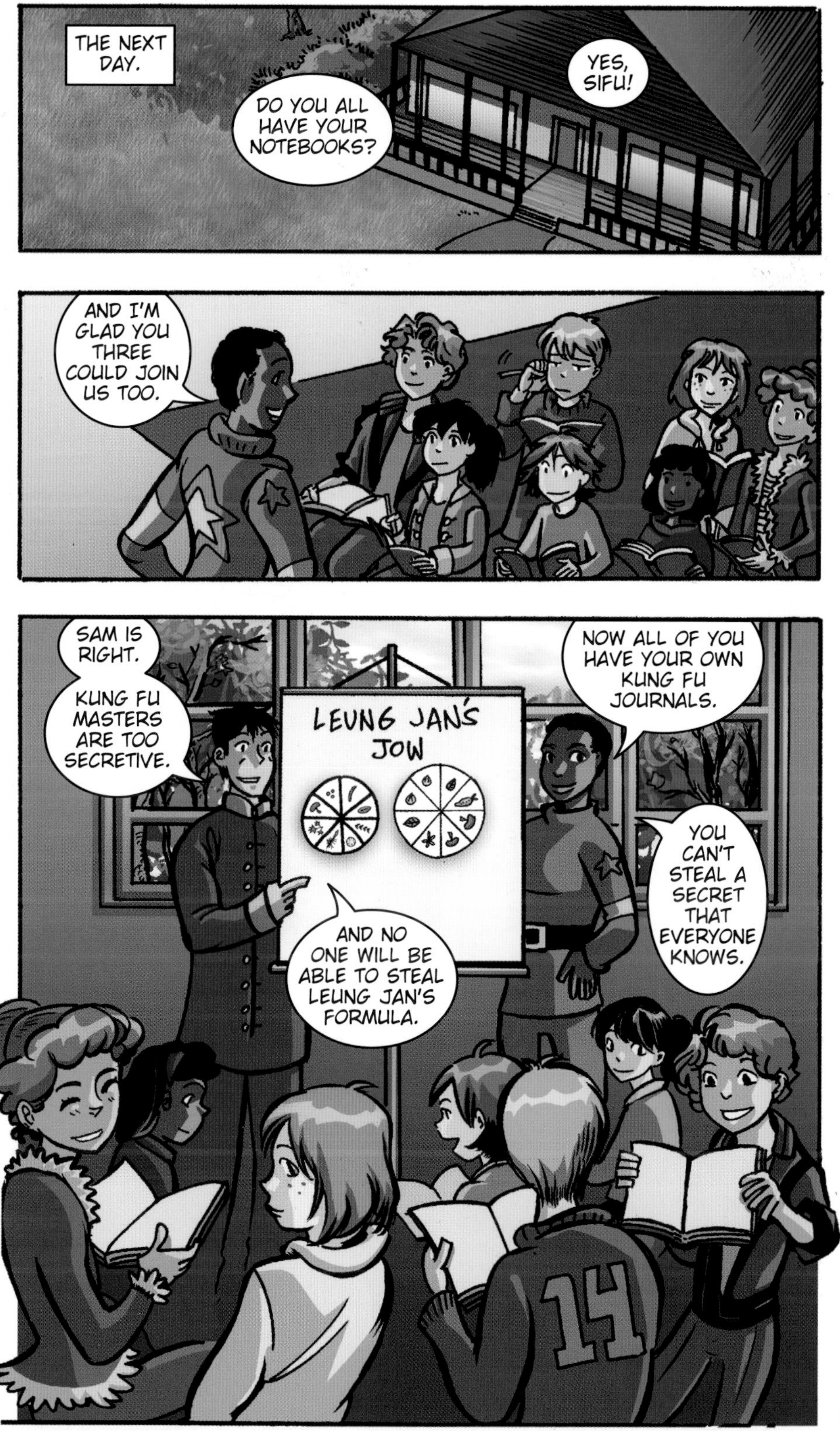
THE NEXT DAY.
DO YOU ALL HAVE YOUR NOTEBOOKS?
YES, SIFU!
AND I'M GLAD YOU THREE COULD JOIN US TOO.
SAM IS RIGHT.
KUNG FU MASTERS ARE TOO SECRETIVE.
LEUNG JAN'S JOW
NOW ALL OF YOU HAVE YOUR OWN KUNG FU JOURNALS.
AND NO ONE WILL BE ABLE TO STEAL LEUNG JAN'S FORMULA.
YOU CAN'T STEAL A SECRET THAT EVERYONE KNOWS.
14

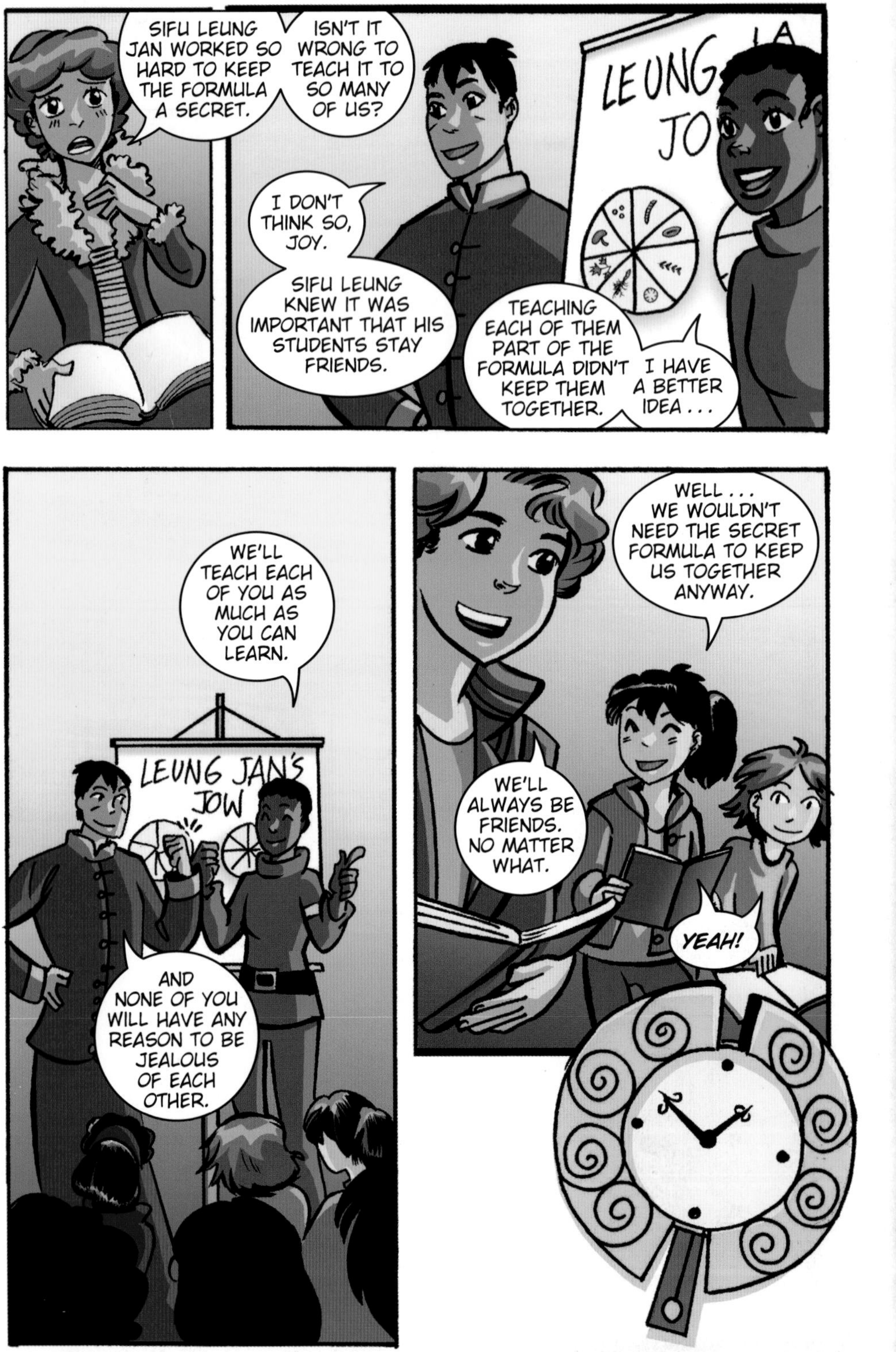
SIFU LEUNG JAN WORKED SO HARD TO KEEP THE FORMULA A SECRET.
ISN'T IT WRONG TO TEACH IT TO SO MANY OF US?
LEUNG
I DON'T THINK SO, JOY.
SIFU LEUNG KNEW IT WAS IMPORTANT THAT HIS STUDENTS STAY FRIENDS.
TEACHING EACH OF THEM PART OF THE FORMULA DIDN'T KEEP THEM TOGETHER.
I HAVE A BETTER IDEA . . .
WE'LL TEACH EACH OF YOU AS MUCH AS YOU CAN LEARN.
LEUNG JAN'S JOW
AND NONE OF YOU WILL HAVE ANY REASON TO BE JEALOUS OF EACH OTHER.
WELL . . . WE WOULDN'T NEED THE SECRET FORMULA TO KEEP US TOGETHER ANYWAY.
WE'LL ALWAYS BE FRIENDS. NO MATTER WHAT.
YEAH!

The Authors

Melinda Thielbar is a teacher who has written math courses for all ages, from kids to adults. In 2005 Melinda was awarded a VIGRE fellowship at North Carolina State University for PhD candidates "likely to make a strong contribution to education in mathematics." She lives in Raleigh, North Carolina, with her husband, author and video game programmer Richard Dansky, and their two cats.

Lydia Barriman is a is a teacher, doctoral candidate, and writer of math courses for all ages.

The Artists

Tintin Pantoja was born in Manila in the Philippines. She received a degree in Illustration and Cartooning from the School of Visual Arts (SVA) in New York City and was nominated for the Friends of Lulu "Best Newcomer" award. She was also a finalist in Tokyopop's Rising Stars of Manga 5.

Yali Lin was born in southern China and lived there for 11 years before moving to New York and graduating from SVA. She loves climbing trees, walking barefoot on grass, and chasing dragonflies. When not drawing, she teaches cartooning to teens.

Becky Grutzik received a degree in illustration from the University of Wisconsin-Stevens Point. In her free time, she and her husband, Matt Wendt, teach a class to kids on how to draw manga and superheroes.

Jenn Manley Lee was born in Clovis, New Mexico. After many travels, she settled in Portland, Oregon, where she works as a graphic designer. She keeps the home she shares with spouse Kip Manley and daughter Taran full of books, geeks, art, cats, and music.

Candice Chow studied animation at SVA and followed her interests through comics, manga, and graphic design. Her previous books include *Macbeth* (Wiley) with fellow SVA graduate **Eve Grandt**, who lives and works in Brooklyn, New York.

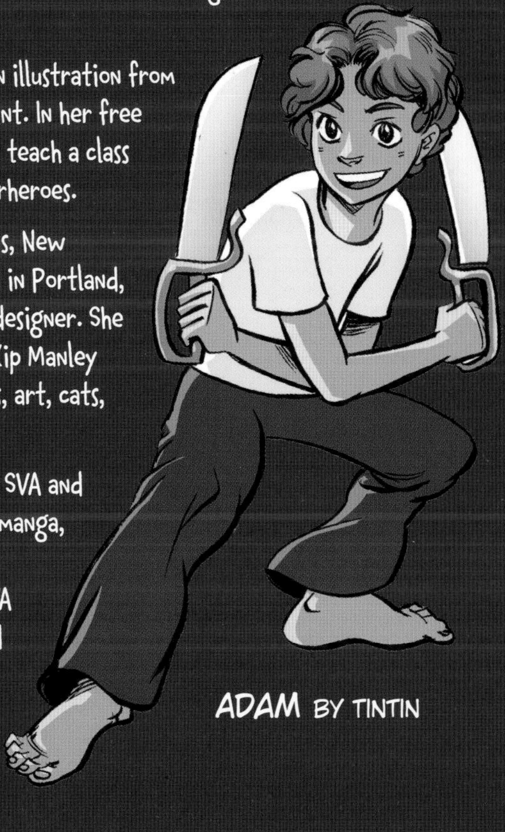

ADAM BY TINTIN

MANGA MATH MYSTERIES #6

It's Stacy's turn to take care of her school's pet fish when somebody pulls a prank. The trickster dumped a complicated concoction of chemicals from the science lab into the fountain, and now the fish are in danger! Stacy and her friends from Sifu Faiza's Kung Fu school must use multiplication and division to solve the who, how, and when behind . . .

THE FISHY FOUNTAIN

JOIN THE KIDS FROM THE KUNG FU SCHOOL IN SOLVING ALL THE MANGA MATH MYSTERIES!

ART BY TINTIN PANTOJA

MANGA MATH MYSTERIES